Rocky Rescue

Sarah Urquhart

Rocky Rescue is a work of fiction. Names, characters, and places are products of the author's imagination or used fictitiously. Any resemblance to locales or persons, living or dead, is coincidental.

Cover design by Untold Designs

This book is a steamy, small town, shifter romance and is for mature audiences only. It contains sexually explicit scenes and adult language that may be offensive to some readers.

Copyright © 2023 Sarah Urquhart

eISBN: 978-1-7388257-2-1

ISBN: 978-1-7388257-3-8

Join my newsletter to keep up to date on new releases, special events, and sneak peeks.

https://bit.ly/3oTgH5u

Also, visit my website at...

http://www.authorsarahurquhart.com

... to see my full book list.

Firebrook Bears Series

Sweet Abandon - Novella

Wild Rescue

Rocky Rescue

Stormy Rescue

Tangled Rescue

For my assistant, Leah. You rock!

Chapter One

B lair walked along the cobbled grey stones of Firebrook's sidewalks, searching everything she passed; not looking for anything—yet—but she didn't want to be found. After checking in to *Bearbrook Cabins*, Blair went in search of groceries to sustain herself for the time here.

Unlike the last time she'd visited Firebrook. A vacation from hell if you ask her. Her best friend's ex and his two chums hadn't come for the vacation.

This trip was all her own. She hated unanswered questions, mysteries with no ending. And everyone had moved on. Not technically, but authorities had lost their interest. Not Blair.

When a who-dun-it murder happened and her best friend became the next victim in line, Blair refused to let that go. Getting thrown into a trunk herself added an extra personal hit.

Blair kept her gaze moving, veering it away from anyone she recognized. Stopping to say hello, giving them the moment to realize who she was, would only send word back to *him*.

The same *him* that sent an ache through her body when she let him enter her thoughts. The one who'd lied to her. It didn't matter that she understood the lie of omission. He still didn't tell her everything when he had the chance.

Slipping into the grocery store, she grabbed a cart and strolled the aisles with her head down. All to avoid him. Poppy had offered to do the shopping for her, but Blair wouldn't have it. The bar she co-owned took up all of Poppy's time. And if not the bar, her mate.

Yeah. Mate. They discovered the world's best kept secret while on vacation. One Blair would happily keep quiet about. She may be an independent reporter, but there were some things the world didn't need to know.

Their vacation landed Poppy in the hands of a bear shifter—her fated mate—after her ex abandoned her on a hike to get rid of her. Firebrook was her home now.

The shifter thing ran through that family. Ran through the town. Wyatt, Poppy's mate, wasn't the only Greer man blessed with the magical ability. His brother. Their two cousins. *Him.*

Blair filled her cart with enough produce for a few days, unsure how well it would last. The rest of her groceries consisted of frozen foods, breads, and easy meats to barbeque. She chose the busiest line at the cash. The town was too small to believe in self-checkout, where she could avoid everyone.

The chit chat of neighbors slowed the line, but when the people behind her joined the conversation in front of her, Blair debated abandoning the store and her food. But the last thing she wanted to be was rude. This town and these people were something special. She'd never seen Poppy as happy as she was now living here.

"See you tomorrow, Jeb." The cashier waved the older man away and turned to Blair. "Good afternoon."

"Hello." Blair smiled and helped push her groceries forward.

Conversation stalled. She was the awkward moment come to life. For today, it suited her purpose. Normally, Blair lived as the boisterous in-your-face and full of questions type of girl. How else could she report stories if she wasn't the first to hear them?

The news station she worked for gave her her own podcast. Once she proved she delivered interesting stories and brought in viewers and listeners without fail, they gave her freedom. *Blairable* quickly became one of the top news podcasts in the country, with a lot of hard work. And had several prerecorded episodes ready to drop while she chased whatever had brought them all to Firebrook. *Them* being two groups of friends. And she used the term friends loosely.

The cashier bagged the groceries as she ran them through, filling three tall paper bags.

"Paper bags, huh? You don't have anything with handles?" She'd chosen to walk. Her tiny car stood out among the pickup trucks and SUVs the locals had to battle the winter roads.

"I'm sorry. I'm all sold out of our reusable bags and our new shipment hasn't come in yet. They've been on backorder for two weeks." The cashier shook her head in disbelief. "We might be an isolated northern town, but we aren't so far north that shipping is often one of our problems."

"Hopefully it doesn't take much longer." Blair stared at the paper bags and made a note to bring her car next time, despite standing out like a shiny thumb.

Blair paid and reached for the bags.

"Oh. Let me get someone to help you out to your car." She lifted a hand to call for someone's attention.

"That's okay. I'm walking." Blair juggled the bags so she carried them three in a row with her arms squeezing around them. She rushed out of the grocery store before anyone else could offer their kind help.

This wasn't like her. Avoiding people and interactions. But since her decision to come back here, she felt like she had one mission.

She smiled and shook her head at all the people who offered to help or offered a ride. She must look ridiculous with only her eyes peering over the tops of the bags. As she walked, the middle bag slipped. Every few steps, she paused and used her knee to hike it back into place.

Sweat beaded at the base of her spine. The summer wasn't quite over. It lingered with a slow and steady retreat while fall woke in the trees. Firebrook was gorgeous in the summer, but with the touches of fall, it turned breathtaking. Those summer temperatures loved the afternoons. And walking with an armload of groceries was more of a workout than she'd like.

"Not as stealthy as you think you are, kitten." *Him.* The voice that called to her every time she closed her eyes heated the back of her neck. The shocking reality of him rather than the echoed imaginings startled her. Her arms loosened enough she dropped her bags.

"Damn it, Noah." Blair followed her bags to the ground and started putting the groceries back in. Noah settled in front of her and lifted her chin. His touch on her skin shocked her as much as his voice. She froze and let him move her face where he wanted it—with her eyes on him. Her lungs trembled.

"You didn't tell me you were coming here."

"Because I didn't want you to know."

"Did you think I wouldn't smell you? This town isn't that big."

Smell. The unsettling reminder of what he was. The big bear shifter would have caught her scent eventually. She'd hoped to at least stay out of his reach.

"What are you doing here, kitten?"

Blair pulled her chin from his grip and packed the soggy cardboard boxes of her not-quite-frozen-anymore groceries. "Shouldn't you be at work? Tourists are still everywhere. I'm sure someone wants to go climb something."

"I was."

Blair stilled. He'd left because he caught her scent. Despite squeezing the promise from Poppy and Wyatt that they wouldn't mention her presence to anyone, she'd known Noah would find her. It didn't matter how much she'd played this encounter out in her mind; she didn't know what to say to him.

What could she say to the one she suspected was her fated mate when he had yet to admit it?

N oah had been replaying their last conversation in his mind for days. For weeks, he'd called her daily after she and her friends left Firebrook. Blair never returned with Poppy when she came back to be with Wyatt. He was happy for his cousin, but Noah hadn't handled his own situation in the best way. Hell, neither of them had. Who knew there were so many ways to fuck up?

Blair had finally answered his call. But when he said he planned to come get her, her parting words were, "Don't bother. I won't be here." He spiraled into a panic and the only thing that kept him from hounding Poppy about her friend was spending his time in the woods as a bear. Fur and dirt kept him sane.

Her scent drifting past on the breeze snapped his focus in two. His bear prowled beneath his skin. *Find her.* He barely had enough attention to speak to Tavis before running into the wind to track her.

"What are you doing here, kitten?"

"You don't sound like you're happy that I'm here." She edged around his question and put the last item in a bag. Lining them up in a row, she squatted low and tried to reach around the base of the bags. Difficult to do with them on the ground.

Noah snatched two bags up and waited for her to grab the third.

"I don't need any help."

"Yes, you do."

"Fine. I don't need *your* help."

He winced, but still didn't give back the bags. "Blair. I'm sorry I didn't tell you everything." The middle of town wasn't the place to have this conversation. The world didn't know about shifters. And this small town he called home didn't know about them either. They wanted to keep it that way.

She didn't answer him, but her lips pinched together while she lifted the third bag and held it on her hip.

"Where are you staying?"

She remained mute.

"I'll find out one way or another. Someone will talk or I'll track your scent."

"At *Bearbrook Cabins*."

"Let's go."

"I said I don't want your help."

Noah crowded into her space. The damn paper bags kept them from touching. "You're getting it anyway, kitten." He'd called her kitten the first time questions flew from her lips with barely a breath in between. Curiosity was vibrant in her very being. It was there now, despite her attempts to hide.

Blair stepped around him and walked toward his cousin's cabins with her chin up high and her attention in one direction. Noah fell into step beside her. The silence of the walk suited him just fine. The words and actions that tingled on his tongue and in his hands weren't appropriate for public ears and eyes.

She led the way past the main lodge and past the cabins until she came to the last one. The smallest one that Caiden, Wyatt's brother, and his mate, Maggie, had been living in until they completed their house. The season had been busy enough that even the small cabin they left open for emergencies filled with tourists.

Blair unlocked the door and walked through the single room. She set her bag on the table and took the others from his arms. After a thunk where they followed the first bag, Blair whirled around and placed both palms on his chest, and pushed. Bracing her feet back, she gave all her might.

"Get out."

She'd moved him back a step when she first laid her hands on him, but now he didn't budge. He couldn't. Her touch tightened everything inside him.

But she continued to shove, her feet doing a stationary slide over the cabin floor.

"Blair." Noah set his hands on her wrists and tilted his head. He kissed her before, and her lips looked like the decadent dessert he remembered. "Stop."

"I can't stop." She closed her eyes. Her pulse raced beneath the pads of his fingers.

Noah pulled her hands away from his chest and up to his shoulders. With all of her weight against him, she would have fallen face first to the floor if he hadn't pulled her up. Flush against his chest, one hand moved down her arm and side to settle on her hip. The other twirled her hair around his finger before tucking it behind her ear.

She stopped fighting him. Desire pooled in her eyes. He'd seen it before.

"I'm going to kiss you, kitten." He lowered his head.

And the fight returned. "No." When she pushed against him this time, she only moved herself back. But either way, he didn't want the space between them.

He reached for her.

"No. Not until you tell me everything."

She knew what he was, what his family was. Bear shifters. His brother and their two cousins. The bakery owner's daughter even found a bear shifter of her own—unrelated to the Greer family. A pack of wolf shifters lived outside of Firebrook. And more shifters lived in towns and cities all around them. Poppy hadn't kept the secret of shifters from her friends when she'd found out she was Wyatt's mate. Blair pieced everything else together herself. That Noah was a shifter, too. That their attraction was more than simple chemistry.

But Noah hadn't confirmed it. She was his mate. And his bear wasn't happy with him at the moment. *Foolish human. Tell her so we can mate her and keep her.*

Blair huffed. "That's what I thought. Now get out." She swung an arm toward the door and turned away from him to put away her groceries.

He swore his bear manifested real claws inside him to swipe against Noah's ribs as he listened to his mate and left her alone.

B lair counted to twenty before letting out the heavy sigh stuck inside her. Her hands trembled as she reached for the groceries, but she didn't have time to steady herself. It may already be too late for some of the frozen foods she'd bought. She read the label of every item she pulled out, mostly as a distraction, and still her mind didn't leave Noah.

All her might hadn't made the man budge. Hard, sharp ridges flexed beneath her palms. The memory of his lips. Hell, she'd missed him. His bossy, overbearing, grumpy nature had been a thorn in her side, but she missed him all the same. From what she'd learned about mates, that may not be her true feelings, but only Fate pushing them together.

But she'd never know for sure or have the chance to process it if that damn man wouldn't admit it.

She wouldn't be back here at all if her curiosity didn't get the better of her. No one knew if Poppy was still in danger. The two who'd murdered Poppy's ex, Scott and Luca, escaped custody and soon after, the safe at the bar Poppy used to work at had been broken into. But nothing on the list of stolen items threw up any red flags. There hadn't been an indecent amount of cash and no valuables. The cops had deemed the theft unrelated to the events in Firebrook. Poppy was the only connection.

Blair's instincts said differently. She didn't think Poppy was the connection at all, but the bar. Her ex had hung around that place more than made sense with the affection he gave Poppy. She'd been their way in, if she'd ever given them the chance.

But the question Blair couldn't answer was, why did they have to come to Firebrook? Poppy's ex had planned their vacation.

There had to have been something else in that safe.

That was the only reason Blair came back. To find what brought them all here. She definitely didn't come back for Noah.

Blair finished with her groceries and then unpacked her suitcase. On most trips, she'd live out of her luggage, but she didn't know how long she would be here and this cabin wasn't big enough to leave her suitcases out.

Poppy insisted Blair come over for supper and a fire tonight. She wouldn't let her friend down. At least she could relax before getting to work. She was starting from scratch with this one, needing to find the missing piece of the puzzle to put it all together, and that meant following tracks. What were Mason, Scott, and Luca doing while in Firebrook?

Grabbing a hoodie, she hung it over her arm while walking to the main lodge.

"All settled in?" Poppy met her halfway.

"Yup. I even unpacked this time."

"Your usual mess wouldn't fit in that cabin."

"You're not wrong." Blair hooked arms with Poppy. The crowd surrounding the barbeque outside of the lodge made Blair pause. A quick scan of the taller heads allowed her to move again. Noah wasn't here.

"Sorry. These things have a life of their own. People smell the barbeque and they show up with their nose in the air. Especially when

Caiden takes over the cooking. I know you wanted to keep a low profile."

"It's okay. I knew it wouldn't last, anyway." She'd let Poppy and Wyatt believe she'd wanted the low profile from everyone, but it was only Noah. And since he wasn't here, she could relax and enjoy her night. The locals were as warm and welcoming as the town itself. Blair didn't mind the people she saw gathering.

Wyatt added wood to the fire that wasn't yet needed for warmth. For a brief instance, he stilled. Straightening, he turned his eyes directly toward Poppy. When Blair looked at her friend, Poppy's gaze was staring back at her mate.

That connection was palpable. Like a physical pulsing between the two people that no one dared cross. Blair could almost see it. And it turned her stomach. Not in a gagging over their public display of affection kind of way, but in a longing jealousy kind of way that only made her feel like a terrible friend.

"He's going to growl loud enough for others to hear soon if you don't get over there." Blair let go of Poppy's arm and nudged her shoulder.

"It's okay. I'm spending time with you. I live with him, remember?"

Blair narrowed her eyes. "Have you seen him at all since this morning?"

"No, but that doesn't matter."

"Go."

Poppy shook her head. "Are you sure?"

"Yes. Go." Blair pushed Poppy in the back and propelled her forward. She saw the moment they both snapped and tuned out everything and everyone around them. Wyatt wrapped his arm around Poppy's waist. Their foreheads touched, and their lips moved, murmuring who knows what kind of sickening delicious things to each other. Then they kissed, and Blair had to look away.

Shaking herself loose, she made her way into the crowd, accepting the hugs from the few people she'd become close enough with the last time she was here. And some she only knew from passing, but hugged her anyway because she was Poppy's friend.

Maggie stood next to Caiden at the barbeque. Bonnie unloaded cookies and cupcakes from the bakery with the help of her husband. No, with the help of her mate. Mate and husband were practically the same, but Blair didn't want to forget the distinction, the part of it that controlled their desires.

Dakota, Wyatt and Caiden's sister, moved from person to person fetching drinks or simply talking.

For something where people just show up, it turned out to be quite the event. Everyone ate, had a few drinks. Some lingered around the fire that continued to roar. Most went home to spend the evening with their families. The community of this place could make anyone's heart burst.

But it wasn't for her.

Wasn't it?

The sun settled, allowing the chill to creep into the air. The fire had a new purpose and everyone was glad it was already blazing hot.

Blair was about to sit on one log to warm up, but she froze. The scene was too familiar. The night she'd sat here with Noah. The night she let him get close.

They'd sat together on that log, alone. Everyone had gone home or back to their cabins. Noah didn't move closer to her, but he wrapped his arm around her to grip her hip and pull her toward him. They'd gotten to know each other that night. Their careers and passions. Their family and friends. Favourite foods and the things that drove them insane. But she hadn't learned the most important part about him. That he was a bear shifter or the reason they were attracted to each other.

But she'd learned how he kissed. Oh, so sweet. At first. Then his lips had commanded her body to submit without words. The measured movements and licks of his tongue had been the first thing to ever quiet her mind.

This memory was the second. Which was why she stared at the log and didn't hear or sense the predator behind her.

Chapter Two

Noah hadn't intended on coming, knowing Blair would be here. But his brother wanted to come and dragged him along under the guise of needing help. As if there weren't enough people here to help him unload new picnic tables.

After leaving her in the cabin, Noah had gone back to work, but tucked himself in the office. He didn't trust his bear not to stalk the outside of the cabin. She'd insisted on space. She'd insisted on answers. Why couldn't he say it? *Blair, you're my mate.* They were only words. Words that determined the rest of their lives. But in the end, it wouldn't matter if he said them or not. She was his mate, and they'd already bonded when she was here the last time. Whenever she crossed his mind, he ached. Muscles throbbed as if he'd run the mountain trails for days in a row. If he felt this much, how was she able to function?

Blair froze by the fire in mid step. Her gaze settled on the log, and her lips parted. Noah knew what she was thinking about. He thought about that night almost every day. That night would have been the perfect opportunity to tell her what he was. But he hadn't.

He stepped up behind her. She was so lost in the memory, she didn't sense him until he reached around her to run his finger along her bottom lip.

"I think about it too, kitten."

Blair gasped, bringing life back into her frozen state.

"Don't move away from me." He bent his head to whisper in her ear. It was a plea. She stayed still, but her head tilted from the log bench to the fire.

"I don't like liars."

"I never lied."

"You left out the truth." She sighed. "I'm sorry. I know why you did. But you should have told me before I left."

"You're right."

Blair's spine snapped straight, and she turned to face him. "I know I'm right."

Noah tore his gaze from her to study the people still present. Too many. "Sit with me?" He nodded at the log.

Blair answered him by sitting. When he sat beside her, their thighs touching, she moved further down.

"Why are you here?"

She remained silent and glared.

"Okay." He gave up. She'd tell him when she wanted, if not before he found out from someone else. She could be here to visit Poppy. But with the way they'd ended their phone call, he suspected she had a different motive. And she wasn't here for him. She made that clear when she kicked him out of the cabin.

"Lots of climbers for the rest of the summer?" She might not be thrilled with their proximity, but she grudgingly made her own effort for small talk.

"Yes. Booked solid. We still have a solid stream booked into the fall."

"That's good. It was fun." Blair and her friends had booked a climbing lesson with them. Noah almost hadn't been able to stand straight, let alone carry equipment and teach. He'd let his brother handle her friends while he kept his focus on the woman who set his insides on fire. His mate.

"Do you want to go again?" Now that he threw the offer out there, he recognized it for the genius idea it was. Get her back in a harness and gripping onto a rock face—at his mercy.

She narrowed her eyes, as if sensing the trap. "Maybe."

"Curious kitten." Noah turned himself sideways and threw a leg over the log to straddle it and face her. "Tomorrow."

"I can't tomorrow." She chewed her lip. "Um, Friday?"

Not saying no, but busy with whatever brought her here. "Friday. Come by in the morning."

"Okay."

Poppy plopped down on the other side of Blair and Wyatt took the spot next to his mate. Being the middle of the week, the crowd hadn't stayed late, but the same group was always left at the end.

Caiden and Maggie hovered for a few moments before saying their farewells. Tavis took over manning the fire. Bonnie snuggled against Easton's chest. Her mate rubbed her back, forcing her to doze after a long day at the bakery. And Dakota chatted animatedly with Poppy, attempting to pull Blair into the conversation.

But Blair's attention was torn. The others may not see it, but Noah did. The small glances, the light breaths. And when she shivered, reaching for her sweater, he waited until she put it on before wrapping his arm around her and pulling her between his legs.

"I'm fine with just my sweater." She tilted her chin down and whispered so her breath brushed his neck.

"I'm not."

"You're cold? Bullshit."

He gave a fake shiver and squeezed his arms tighter. Her teeth biting the inside of her cheek didn't hide the light lift to the corners of her lips. It was progress. He may not understand how to bring to words what she already knew, but he didn't want the space between them.

Easton lifted a sleeping Bonnie and nodded to each of them. The other bear fit in well, despite being unrelated. Dakota and Tavis paused in their conversation to throw identical looks at the couples on the log. Without an explanation, they left. No one else was paying attention to them, anyway. Noah tracked everyone around them, waiting for the moment he and Blair were alone.

"Mack gets up too early for my liking. I need to get some sleep." Poppy stood with the help of Wyatt and turned to Blair. "Want us to walk you back to the cabin?"

Noah gave a slight shake of his head for Wyatt to interpret.

"I'm sure Noah can walk her back." Wyatt set his hands on Poppy's hips to steer her toward the lodge. Poor Blair didn't have a chance to answer anyone as Wyatt and Poppy ambled across the lawn.

She turned around, facing him. The fire had heated her skin, giving her the same glow she'd had the last time they'd been here alone.

"Let me kiss you, kitten."

She followed the slow shake of her head with a hand on his chest. He was sure her intention had been to keep distance between them, but her fingers dug into his muscles.

"Then let me touch you."

"You already are."

"I'm holding you. This." He lifted his hand and ran the back of his knuckle down her cheek. "This is touching." Turning his hand, he used the tip of his finger to trace the same path and move lower. Along her jaw. Down her neck, and dipping ever so slightly in the collar of her sweatshirt.

The only other sound that cut through their loud breaths was the crackle of the dying fire. Noah continued to trace her jaw and neck until he saw her pulse race at the base of her throat. His hand at her hip gripped tight, contrast to the light touch of his fingers.

Her eyes closed for a moment, but when she opened them, they were wide with an awareness that hadn't been there for most of the night.

"No. This isn't real." She tried to back away from him, but he wasn't ready to let go yet.

"What do you mean, Blair? This is very real."

She pushed harder against him and he let her go. "Is it? Or does this have to do with the thing you still won't tell me?"

"Ask me." The words wouldn't come to him on their own, but maybe if she forced them from him, they could move past this.

"And make it easy for you? No." Blair stood and stalked toward her cabin.

"Blair. I'll walk you. Let me put out the fire." He reached for the bucket of sand, but Blair never stopped.

She picked up at a jog as she called back to him. "Don't bother."

Fuck. She'd seen through him so well. But with so many opportunities to tell her wasted, it wouldn't take a genius to guess he was having trouble with words.

He put out the fire and walked up to Blair's cabin. The light was low on the inside from a lamp, but he didn't see her. He didn't knock on the door or move toward a window. Knowing she'd made it inside and safe was enough.

A wild hum moved through him. His bear growled at him once again for being so stupid, as if to say, *put me in charge. I'll get the job done.*

If Noah didn't own up to the truth soon, his bear would do it for him.

Blair locked the door of the cabin behind her. She had her tote loaded with her tablet, her phone, wallet, and notepad. She may have wanted a low profile to avoid Noah as long as she could, but that time was over. He'd discovered her, touched her, and forced her dreams into a fever.

It was time to work her social magic and talk to people. Starting with the owner of the cabins they'd stayed in last time.

The town centre bustled. She recognized the same locals setting up displays in their windows and outside their stores. Tourists oohed and aahed as they passed by. The smells from all the restaurants and coffee shops made most people detour from their destination. Blair already had the bakery set in mind for her first stop.

Bonnie smiled brightly from behind the counter at each person who approached her. She called out the drink orders for someone else to make while she dished up the baked goods made by her and her mother, continuing the conversation with the customers while she did it.

Blair was the last in line. When she reached the counter, Bonnie paused and leaned her arms over the glass cabinet containing the pastries.

"Hey. How are you this morning?" Bonnie leaned her chin on her hands.

"Good, but in desperate need of coffee." She didn't need to tell Bonnie how restless her sleep had been.

"You want something sweet or the straight stuff?" The twitch of her lips made Blair think she saw the exhaustion tugging at her.

"The extra sugar wouldn't hurt. Something with peppermint, please." Blair shrugged.

Bonnie turned her head over her shoulder to speak to the teenager working behind her. "Can you make a large white chocolate peppermint latte, please?"

"Sounds like the wrong season." Blair would be all over that at Christmas.

"We keep all our drinks going all year round. I'll push certain flavours in different seasons, but this particular drink is one of our most popular. Especially in the evenings."

"Thank you."

"Sorry I fell asleep last night. I've been so drained lately."

"You didn't miss much. Everyone left soon after."

"You and Noah were getting awfully cozy." Anyone else would draw that statement out with a raised brow and a shoulder wiggle. But Bonnie's smile tilted and her eyes narrowed. She was the mate to a bear shifter and knew herself this wasn't a simple attraction.

"I wouldn't let him walk me back to the cabin and ran off while he dealt with the fire." Maybe sometime soon, Blair would go to Poppy and Bonnie for advice on how to handle everything going on inside her. How was she supposed to determine what was real and what was magic?

"Ha. I bet he didn't take that well. He might be grumpy from time to time, but manners like those are ingrained in him. Not walking you back to the cabin must have gone against his very being."

"He didn't sound happy."

The teenager passed Blair her drink over the glass cabinet.

Blair wrapped her fingers around the hot cup and moved toward the cash register.

"You want anything to eat with that?"

"No, thank you. I might swing by for lunch, though."

"Make it an early one and I might join you." Bonnie rang up the coffee on the register. Blair paid and lifted her coffee in farewell before emerging onto the busy sidewalk.

Blair kept her eyes up, picking out the locals from the tourists. Of course, she didn't know everyone and couldn't always be sure, but it hadn't taken long during their vacation to spot the difference. A block away from the bakery, she saw one place she'd planned to avoid until she'd talked to Noah last night.

Rockhard Bears had several groups of people milling about outside while Tavis and Noah each led a group around the building. Noah paused. He whipped his head around in her direction.

Pulling in a painful gasp, Blair looked away. She'd slapped her gaze ahead of her and jogged across the street, making her rush seem as if she didn't want to hold up the cars waiting to go. The way her spine tingled said he still hadn't looked away. Several deep breaths later, and the feeling was gone.

The busy street had thinned the further she got away from the town centre and *Rockhard Bears*. The cabins they'd stayed at while here earlier in the summer weren't anything like the ones Poppy's mate owned. These looked like a broken apart motel. The owners put so much love and care into them they created a homey atmosphere, but with neighbors close enough to shake hands from their doorsteps.

Wyatt and Caiden put distance between each of their cabins to give guests privacy. But they had the space and land to do that.

The vacancy and open signs sat side by side in the window of the main office. Blair walked in with a smile. Millie sat behind the counter.

"Hello. What can I do for you?"

"I don't suppose you remember me. I stayed here with friends in June."

Millie narrowed her eyes before her smile replaced her thoughts. "Yes, I think I do. You came in two groups, didn't you?"

Blair gave her a pinched nod. The guys had stayed in one cabin while Blair, Poppy, and Harlyn stayed in another. The guys had trashed the cabin the girls had stayed in and hid out in their own after they'd killed Mason.

"How are you doing, dear?" Millie stood up, her rings clinking as she clasped her hands together on the desk.

"I'm doing well, thank you. I hope our stay didn't hurt your business for the summer."

"Not for long. Don't you worry." Millie waved a hand in front of her. "Is there something I can do for you? Are you looking for a place to stay again?"

"No. I came by to talk to you about what happened in June."

"Oh?"

"Do you mind if I ask you a few questions?"

"Certainly, but I'm not sure how much help I can be."

"That's okay. We only did a few things with them on the trip. Do you know where they spent their time? Did they ever ask you for directions anywhere?

"No. I can't say they did. Herb?" She whirled around so her voice echoed toward the office in the back.

"Yes?" He poked his head out and looked at his wife, but his gaze fell to Blair. "Well, hello."

Blair smiled in return.

"You remember the group here in June?" She didn't wait for him to answer, but kept asking her questions. "Did any of the boys ask you for directions anywhere?"

"Not that I recall. But that doesn't happen very often anymore."

"It doesn't." Millie confirmed. "In a digital age, tourists use online maps and directions rather than ask their host." A sad smile followed her half shrug.

Blair turned toward the husband. "Do you remember where they went while they were here? Any places they visited stand out?"

Herb's thicker brows drew together, and he took a few minutes to think through his answer. "I don't know where exactly, but I saw them in different places around town. Not always a place I expect to see tourists, but sometimes they venture everywhere."

"Like where?"

"Around some neighborhoods. Just walking by though."

"Thank you." Blair gave them her brightest smile. They were a sweet couple and didn't deserve what happened at their place of business. She'd seen the pride they had in their cabins and in the town they called home. "If you think of anything else, please call me?"

"Of course." Millie pulled out a pad of paper and a pen, pushing it across the counter. Blair wrote her name and number down.

"Thanks again. Have a great day."

"You too, dear."

Blair walked out of the office. The heat of his eyes skated over her before she saw him. And it took running into his hard chest to realize how close he was.

He was going to owe the family waiting for him an apology. Noah had spotted Blair going into Millie and Herb's, and he abandoned the group waiting to gather gear and head out for a climbing lesson. But he had to ask her again.

"What are you up to?" Noah set his hands on Blair's shoulders, holding her in one spot. Not against him and not away from him.

"Don't sneak up on me." Blair breathed deep and closed her eyes, as if startled.

"Answer me, Blair." He made circles over the exposed skin from her tank top with his thumbs.

Disgust curled her nose and her eyes opened, narrowing on him in an instant. "No. I don't owe you any answers, especially when you demand like that." Blair shrugged out of his hold.

"Damn it. You are the kitten I've named you, aren't you? Are you digging into what happened in June?" He knew the passion she held for getting answers. But digging into this when the murderers were loose and had gone after Poppy—hell, they'd stuffed Blair and Harlyn in a trunk—was reckless.

"Why would I do that? Scott and Luca are in the wind and the police have said there's nothing else to find." Blair walked around him and paused long enough to check for traffic before crossing the road. Noah caught up to her.

"Don't."

"Don't what, Noah?" She added a jaunt to her stride as she continued to walk away with her gaze on anything but him.

"Blair." He grabbed her elbow to swing her around to face him. With little resistance, she landed against him.

"Tell me." She challenged, tilting her head back to line up her nose and chin with his. "Because otherwise, you have no say in what I do."

Noah huffed. "I don't believe for a second you'd listen if I tell you that you're my...." The final word swelled in his throat, gripping the sides to keep him from expelling it. His hold on her elbow loosened.

"You can't even say it hypothetically." Blair shook her head and stepped back. "You have a family waiting for you." She looked across the street where the family he'd abandoned waited out front of *Rock-hard Bears.*

Fuck. He smiled and waved at the parents, giving a nod to say he'd be there soon, but when he turned back to Blair, she was already several feet away. Dealing with her would have to wait.

Jogging across the road, he approached the family. "Very sorry about that. Let's get this show on the road." He grinned down at the kids who'd been the most excited about the climbing adventure. Most kids were, until they started climbing. Many realized their fear of heights during their first climbing lesson. Others took time to adjust before finding a love for the sport. And adrenaline that fueled them any time they left the ground.

Leading them around back, he gathered the gear and fit them all for harnesses. For the next couple of hours, Noah focused on the family and not on his bear pacing back and forth inside him. Anger heated the animal's eyes that hovered behind his own.

After waving the family off, he thought he had time to track down Blair, but Tavis walked in with a new group. Tavis gave him an odd frown. He likely sensed the tension coming from Noah. But he still passed the young couple on their honeymoon off on him.

As mad as he wanted to be, this was their business—the livelihood they'd built together. Telling his bear to calm the fuck down wasn't easy, but he did it to get through the rest of the day.

When the last customer left, his brother trapped him while they locked up the equipment for the night.

"What's up with you?" Tavis didn't look up from the rope he coiled around his arm.

"Blair's back in town."

Tavis paused. "I know. Did you forget I was at the barbeque last night, too?"

"No, but you asked what was wrong."

"So it's Blair?"

Noah stopped what he was doing and stared at his brother, who was being dense to coax Noah to talk.

"You're difficult to deal with on the best of days."

"Gee, thanks man," Noah drawled and rolled his eyes.

"But since they left, you've had some really bad days. I've wanted to say something. Something we've all suspected."

"Don't." Noah heard the question his brother was about to ask, and if anyone was going to ask him, he wanted it to be Blair. He wouldn't give the answer to anyone but her.

"Noah." Tavis stopped everything he was doing, setting all the equipment down to square off with Noah.

"I said don't." His bear escaped in his voice that time. That always made each other pause. If one or the other was upset enough it drew out the animal inside them, they backed off.

Tavis said nothing else, but he didn't back off. Crossing his arms, he blocked Noah's path.

"Leave it alone, Tavis." Noah reined his bear back in. The last thing he wanted was to get into a fight with his brother. Not because he was incapable of a few simple words.

"Fine. But deal with it before you take it out on someone who doesn't deserve it." Tavis left and Noah finished the clean up alone. Alone with his thoughts. And alone with his bear.

Chapter Three

*A*round some of the neighborhoods didn't give Blair much to work with. But it told her they hadn't been here for the tourist activities. They'd done a couple things with the girls, a hike where Poppy got left behind, and they'd tried to do rock climbing together.

Blair paused. Noah had refused the guys when they'd all gone in, stating the reservation only said for three. It had been a lie, one they'd been thankful for. But had the guys gone back for their own lesson? The one person she was avoiding could answer that. He wasn't the only one, though. His brother. Was it possible to track down one without the other?

But first, she needed her daily shot of caffeine. There were other locals willing to help her before she tracked down any Greer men.

Inside *Bella's Bakery*, Blair ordered her coffee from Bonnie and asked if she had a couple of minutes.

"For you? Yes." The other woman beamed and spoke to the people working behind her. She stepped out from behind the counter and joined Blair at the small two person table sitting in the back corner of the bakery. "Everything okay?"

"Of course."

"That's good. The way you asked and chose this dark corner made me wonder." Bonnie let her eyes dart conspiratorially around the room.

"Everything is fine, but I have a question for you." Blair took a slow sip of her coffee.

"Shoot."

Leaning in, she set her elbows on the table and wrapped her hands around her cup. "You remember the guys we were here with in the summer?"

"People around here won't forget those faces for a while," Bonnie scoffed.

"Did you ever see where they went or what they did while they were here?" She needed the eyes of the nosy locals to kick off this search.

"Oh." Bonnie frowned while staring at the table. She chewed on the inside of her lip while she thought. "Not that I can remember. They came in here a few times."

"Okay. Who might have seen them?"

Bonnie narrowed her eyes, catching onto Blair's plans. "Why?" The single word stretched out as she lowered her tone.

"I'm just trying to connect some dots." Blair gave a half smile and tried to wave it all away.

"Bullshit." Bonnie quirked a single brow and waited for Blair to confirm her theory. Which she did with a blush. "What are you up to?"

"I'm trying to connect more than dots. I want to know what they're up to. They're still in the wind, and something brought them to Firebrook." She left out the words, *this isn't over.*

Bonnie shook her head with a long sigh. "You better be careful."

"This isn't my first time doing this." Maybe her first time on this level. Chasing murderers wasn't yet on her resume.

"Why does that not surprise me?" Bonnie smiled. "I'm not sure who, but I'd start with all the major businesses on this street. Like I said, not many have forgotten them so soon. They'll know who you're talking about and if they have anything to say about them, they'll gladly tell you."

"Thank you." Blair squeezed Bonnie's hand before leaving, her coffee in hand.

She had two different directions to go—one that may have more information and another so vague she didn't know where to start.

Blair spent the next several hours going in and out of businesses on the main street running through town only to come out with nothing. Bonnie had been right about one thing. People were more than willing to talk. But none had remembered where they'd gone.

She'd been shuffling her feet along the pavement when she reached *Poppy Mack's*, the bar Poppy co-owned since moving to Firebrook. The sign on the front door said closed, but Blair knocked anyway. Mack, Poppy's partner, peered through the window before opening the door.

"I'd remind you that we're closed, but I assume you belong to Poppy." Mack grunted and opened the door wider.

"Thank you." Blair walked inside and found Poppy sitting at the bar, sorting through papers. Mack moved behind the bar, picking up a rag he threw over his shoulder.

"Hey. What brings you by?" Poppy glanced up from her papers with a smile, but Blair saw her attention was tethered to her work.

"Just needed a quiet breather." Blair leaned on the shining bar top with her elbows.

"Not getting very far?" Poppy flipped the top page over upside down on a new pile.

"Not really. Everyone loves to talk, but there aren't any answers or directions in what they're saying."

"Well, what do you have so far?" Poppy stood and leaned over the counter, motioning for Mack to hand her a bottle she pointed to on the back wall. Pulling up a glass from under the counter, she took the bottle from Mack, who shook his head with a frown. Poppy poured Blair half a glass of wine and glanced at the next paper in her pile.

"That they were seen walking about neighborhoods. That came from Herb. And everyone else had been sure the trio was up to no good the second they rolled into town." Blair rolled her eyes. "They'd all forgotten that there had been six of us and not just the three of them." She sipped at her drink and sighed.

"You've only just started. Patience." Poppy looked away from her work long enough to squeeze Blair's shoulder. "If anyone is persistent enough, it's you."

If it was only the mystery hovering over her head, Blair wouldn't feel so drained from only a day of asking questions. She'd be invigorated and determined. But Noah also hovered. Over her head, at her shoulders, on her mind, in her dreams, and everywhere she looked.

Mack stopped shining the glassware and stopped in front of Blair on the other side of the bar. "I shouldn't tell you this." He paused. Blair didn't dare question him because she felt he was about to say it anyway and didn't want to change his mind. "You shouldn't be asking questions after someone who's capable of murder and still out there."

Blair bit her tongue. Disappointment was as sharp as her teeth. She'd hoped he'd had a lead. Not a warning.

"I saw them on Brenton Road a few times."

She locked her wide, grateful eyes on the older man. "Thank you."

"You best be careful." Mack's growl faded as he turned back to the glassware.

"I always am."

Poppy choked and tried to clear her throat.

"Doubtful." Mack glared over his shoulder.

"What's on Brenton Road?" Blair looked at both Poppy and Mack.

"A church, the library, municipal owned buildings." Mack didn't look up from where he spun the towel inside an already dry glass. The man seemed to fidget to keep himself busy.

Blair frowned. What were they looking for in places like a library or church? One way to find out. Outside these doors that hid her so well.

Noah spent most of the night in fur and stalking the woods around Blair's cabin. It had been enough to appease the animal so he could focus on work. The tourists were still plentiful enough they were busy. He didn't have time to chase after Blair.

Every minute of the morning that his mind thought of her soft and sweet curves, her eyes that looked at everything with wonder, or the attitude she wrapped around her shoulders with confidence, Noah growled and found something new to do. Focus on the next client, clean the floors, reorganize already well organized equipment. Anything so her face didn't enter his mind or her scent floating through town didn't pull him away from their business again.

By noon, Tavis sent him away. "Go take care of this. You don't want to talk about it, but you need to deal. The family you taught this morning didn't exactly complain, but they made a comment."

"They made a comment? What kind of comment?"

"They asked if you were okay. They said you seemed like you were having a bad day. They'd heard so many nice things about us from friends that they assumed this wasn't normal behaviour for either of us. Go fix this before we get real complaints."

This was their business, and they ran it as they saw fit. If that meant being rude to certain customers or turning others away, they did it without hesitation. But those scenarios didn't happen often. And being rude to a kind family who listened to every instruction was unacceptable.

Noah hadn't even noticed his mood. He'd only been going through the motions.

"I'll find out where they're staying and apologize."

"I'm sure they'd appreciate that." Tavis pointed to the door. "I'm here if you change your mind and want to talk. But I doubt you have much more time to get things straightened out before the pain hits."

His brother referred to what happened to mates if they fought Fate. Pain seeped into their bodies. Some became ill. Noah denied the aches since Blair first left town. Now that she'd returned, he felt close to normal. Close.

It must be his imagination that his heart beat harder and faster since he first caught her scent two days ago. That his ribs ached with the extra effort from the muscle. That the base of his skull throbbed with magic that hurt when he tried to fight it. The one thing he couldn't bring himself to say.

Noah conceded to his brother and left. This wasn't fixable in an afternoon.

But to start, he had to get Blair to talk to him.

There, waltzing out of *Poppy Mack's* bar, shoulders back, chest out, and tired eyes that said more than a mystery plagued her. Shadows extended further down her cheeks than they had the last time he'd seen her.

"Blair." He called out to her and saw her tense before she turned around.

"Might as well get this over with while I have the chance." The muttered words reached him seconds before he reached her. She turned around with pursed lips and her head tilted. "I have a question for you." Blair spoke as if she'd been the one to call out to him.

He'd take it. "What's your question?"

He'd surprised her by acquiescing. Her head tilted back, and she stuttered before getting her voice to come out even. "Did the guys ever come back and reschedule a climbing lesson?"

Noah closed the distance between them, towering over her. "You are not chasing after them."

A slow rise lifted her chin. "I can ask your brother."

"Blair…" He trailed off from a warning he shouldn't give. Fuck, she walked a dangerous path.

"Noah." Her voice leveled in a lower tone that didn't challenge like he supposed she planned. No, it stroked its way down his body.

"I don't want you to get hurt." The honesty crept from him. Blair's lips parted and some of the fight left her eyes.

"I'll be fine."

Noah held her gaze the way he wanted to hold her. After a deep breath, he answered her. "No. They never came back. But we weren't friendly, so I never expected them to."

He watched her attention fold in on itself. Her face turned down while her mouth twisted as if she chewed on nothing. She pondered his answer more than her irritation of being in his presence.

"Kitten." It had been the wrong thing to say to get her attention.

Fierce eyes pulled her out of her thoughts and slapped themselves onto him.

"Blair. I'd like to ask you something, too." He controlled his tone, not giving her a reason to snap back at him.

"What?"

"Will you have dinner with me tonight?"

Blair took a full step back, and he cursed the space. But Noah stayed in place, as if not reaching for her extended a sign of good faith.

When she didn't answer, he needed to fill the silence. Not a usual problem for him. "Please, Blair."

"Okay." But she took another step back with her answer.

"I'll pick you up."

"No. I'll meet you. Where?"

Noah hadn't been raised that way, but if it was what she needed to agree, he'd allow it. "My place."

Blair narrowed her eyes. "Try again."

"We need to talk. We can't talk in public."

Her breath caught. She took a few minutes before she nodded. Turning away, she left before he said more. He didn't have more to say, anyway. Not that he could say in the street or that she would want to hear from him.

Noah watched her until she turned a corner. Walking toward the grocery store, he ticked off ideas of what to make her. Caiden was the cook of the family, but Noah had a few things he made well.

Then he needed to practice saying the words aloud. The words everyone knew were true, but couldn't escape his throat.

B lair had given up her search two hours into the afternoon. Her thoughts circled back to Noah. His entire demeanor had changed as he'd approached her outside of Poppy's bar. Well, after he'd finished scolding her.

He'd tried. That alone made her wonder if she'd get some answer from him tonight. But even that possibility wasn't enough to dampen her frustration with him for distracting her. Distracting her enough to abandon her search and go back to the cabin to shower and get ready for a date. A damn date with a bear. It pissed her off. Despite her body lighting up at the idea of being alone with him.

The attraction pulsed. Every time his name crossed her mind. Every time his voice filled her ear or his nearness scalded her skin. And the static of that attraction zapped her as she walked up the plain path of stones to his front door.

It was a small house, with no more than two bedrooms. The front deck looked to be almost as big as the main floor. A long swing looked inviting as it moved with the breeze. She hadn't expected to see something so welcoming from the grumpy, overbearing man.

She paused at the bottom of the steps as the door opened. Right. Bear shifter. He would have heard her coming. Or smelled her. These traits of shifters she'd learned from Poppy. Not Noah. He hadn't denied it, but they seemed to be things he had trouble admitting.

Noah filled the doorway. A soft, clean T-shirt pulled taut over his torso while dark jeans covered his legs. His hair, that had an obvious attempt at being combed, still sat tousled over his head. But the scruff on his jaw grew a little more with each day she'd been here. He cleaned up nice. Too nice.

"Come on in, kitten." His voice made her heart skip a beat. The sound, somehow grumpy, didn't match his lopsided grin as he held the door.

Blair took the steps with caution. Not because of him, but because her muscles weakened as she took him in.

"You look good." His voice travelled down from her shoulder as she stepped past him. She'd brought more than enough clothes to last her for however long she stayed in Firebrook, so it hadn't been hard to pick out a simple long-sleeved dress.

"So do you." She mimicked his grumble, adding her own feminine purr. Entirely unintentional, but his proximity seemed to control parts of her she wished it didn't. He shut the door behind her and held out his arm to gesture toward the open space of his house. A half wall behind the counter separated the kitchen and living room. The wood on top was larger and finished with a bar top shine.

"It's not big."

"It doesn't need to be." Blair had a thing for comfortable and cozy atmospheres. She might love the bustle of people, work, and friends, but a home was different. The furniture was all leather and large enough to fit his frame. Pictures of him and his family, the rest of the Greer clan, hung on the walls and sat on the end tables. Down the hall were four doors. She thought she'd been right about there only being two bedrooms.

"Can I get you something to drink?" He faced her. She warmed under his gaze, but there was something off with the way he spoke. Like every word took effort.

"Whatever you're having is fine." Blair sipped fine wine with elites or tipped back homemade beer with the rednecks. And she found she liked most anything she had.

He passed her a bottle. "Have a seat. Dinner will be ready soon."

"Did you cook?" She asked softly, with no surprise. His cousin was a brilliant chef, after all.

"I hope you like chili." Again, his words seemed clipped, but his face relaxed and the tension between them was as palpable as ever.

"I do." Blair sat at the bar. Noah moved to the other side and pulled rolls out of a plastic bag to cut and butter.

"How was your afternoon?"

Blair had to stop herself from snorting at the question. Then she looked at him. He was trying so hard to be polite. She saw it now, the reason he sounded almost odd.

"Blair?"

She'd been staring. "Well, not great. I got distracted."

His lips twitched and the sides of his eyes crinkled for only a second. "Oh? Distracted with what?"

"This and that." Blair didn't need to give him details or her own thoughts. Not until he admitted everything to her.

"And what were you doing this afternoon?"

"This and that." They'd been over this. And as things stood, it wasn't any of his business.

It was almost comical to watch his jaw lock and unlock as he held back what he really wanted to say. "Have you done anything fun since coming back? Are you looking forward to climbing again on Friday?"

"I am." Even without Noah constantly at her back, she would have enjoyed it.

"Good."

She couldn't take any more of it. Why he acted so polite was beyond her. "So, you wanted to talk?"

"I didn't ask you over just to talk." The sound of his voice warmed and had lost the strict politeness.

"Okay, a date. To talk," she pushed.

"Yes, we need to talk, but that isn't the only reason you're here." The slip didn't last long.

"Why did you ask me to come?"

"I wanted to spend time with you." A small growl followed his words.

A timer dinged on the stove and Noah turned from her to tend to the pot. His shoulders moved with deep breaths, as if getting himself under control. He pulled down bowls and started scooping out the chili. He'd already set a small table on the other side of the kitchen near the front window, looking out onto his deck. Before taking the dishes to the table, he came around to the other side of the bar and held a beefy hand out to her.

Hers looked so small next to his. She wasn't a tall woman, but she never felt small when walking into a room. Unless Noah was there.

Blair slid her hand in his and pressed her lips together to hold back her gasp. He pulled her from the stool and took her to the table. "Where have these manners been?"

Noah paused. "I'm sorry if I haven't..."

Blair couldn't do it. She laid her hand on his arm to stop him. "I'm teasing, Noah."

"No, I've been overbearing." He held a chair for her.

"It might help if you tell me why you've been over*bear*ing." Blair threw in the fitting joke for good measure and it helped. He'd lost the guilt that hardened his face after she'd teased him. He wasn't wrong.

He'd been pushy since she returned and even some when she'd been here last time, but he never crossed any lines. She'd seen him use the same manners toward others in the community. Noah was a genuinely honorable man. Blair could only tease him so far.

He returned with the two bowls, then went back for the rolls.

"This isn't your cousin's recipe." She stared at the bowl in awe. They'd had the chili at Caiden's restaurant before. It was delicious, but this was amazing.

"No. It's mine."

"It's better." On a whole other level.

"I know." The smug grin gave the grumpy man a charming boyish look that did odd things to her.

"Does he know?" Blair spooned another bite.

"Yes. And it drives him crazy." Thrill entered Noah's eyes. He loved that it bothered Caiden.

"And you wouldn't help a cousin out?" Blair tilted her head and held back her laugh while she picked up a roll.

"Not with this."

The rest of dinner was quiet, but that didn't stop her ears from ringing with every look they passed each other. The heat intensified, and the tension grew taut. Swallowing became difficult.

Blair took a long drink of her beer to smooth out her throat. He copied the motion. Eventually, they both finished and pushed their bowls away.

"We could go for a walk. Or watch a movie." He smiled with his suggestions.

"So you can sneak your arm around my shoulders?" Blair stood from the table.

"I don't need to sneak." He stood, too.

"Oh? You have moves, do you?" She turned toward him. They weren't close enough to touch each other, but another couple of inches and she would have brushed against him. His eyes dropped down her body.

Noah cleared his throat and lifted the dishes from the table. "Another drink?" The man was trying so hard. Every time she'd seen him since coming back, he'd found some reason to touch her, even hold her.

"Sure. Thanks." The distance bothered her. The heat in her core simmered, never dying or growing brighter. She followed him into the kitchen.

He passed her the drink and smiled.

"Noah." She ran her hand up his arm.

He stiffened. "We should talk." But that same stiff arm reached for her. His hand rested on her hip and he curled his fingers to urge her closer.

Blair couldn't not touch him. She was still mad that he'd left so much out, but now that they were alone again, her hold on the attraction snapped. Just as it had by the fire. She waited for the moment reality would retake control. Blair wanted him to talk, to tell her everything, yet she ran her finger in circles on his chest.

"Blair." He set his beer down and used that hand to grip her wrist. He didn't stop her, but moved with her. "You wanted me to talk."

"I still want you to talk." Blair discovered she had a war of her own going on inside her. Attraction fought for dominance over the reasons she knew she needed to hold out.

"It's hard enough on its own. Even worse, with you touching me."

"I don't want to stop." He was so hard under her hands.

"Then I won't be talking." A growl rumbled at the base of each word. She'd never heard someone sound quite like that. Only Noah.

"Oh, I really hope you do." She imagined all the raw things he'd say during intimacy.

The growl deepened and dropped to his chest. His grip changed, and he pinned her against the counter. Blair set her beer down and gripped his shoulders. She'd tempted him and now she had to pay the price.

Chapter Four

He had to pat himself on the back for lasting as long as he had. Noah pinned Blair against the counter and gloried in his body pressing into hers. This wasn't how tonight was supposed to go. He'd had every intention of baring it all to her and giving her the confirmation to what she already knew.

A simple date and time spent together turned into a short, awkward night of tension that bubbled between them. It seemed he wasn't the only one who snapped.

Blair had been so mad and firmly set in what she thought was reality, different from the attraction between them. But her breathing sped up and her touch heated the same way his did.

Noah refused to let her regret this decision. She'd walked—no, she ran—from him the last time they were this close, convinced this wasn't real.

"Put your hands on the counter." He issued the rhythmic command, surprised she obeyed. Noah needed her to let go of him so he could let go of her. Taking steps back, he kept going until she was out of his reach.

"Noah?"

"Talk first, kitten."

Her fists tightened around the edge of the counter, turning her knuckles white. "We have all night to talk. Don't we?"

"We do. But I don't want you to regret anything."

Blair shook her head and pushed off the counter. Walking past him, her arm brushed his, but she took her beer and walked around the half wall to the living room.

Noah grabbed his own drink and swallowed half of it. The alcohol didn't affect shifters as easily as it did humans, but that didn't stop him from swallowing it hard to give him the pseudo effect of liquid courage.

He followed Blair into the living room. She already settled on the couch, her legs crossed and leaning on her forearm. Noah couldn't sit. He stood in front of her and took a deep breath.

"You know what I am."

"I do? What are you?"

He narrowed his eyes and wondered if the others had this same difficulty saying the words aloud to their mates. To say something that had been a strict secret for almost his entire life physically strained his lungs.

"I can b*ear*ly stand the excitement." Blair bit her lip and continued to wait while he struggled in front of her.

Noah lowered his chin and swallowed.

"Need me to count down for you?"

"No. This is harder than I imagined. It's been a secret for so long."

Her face softened. "I understand." But then a grin lifted her lips. "I'll count and then you just spit it out, don't think."

Noah didn't trust that smile.

"Ready. Teddy. Go."

He scoffed. "You aren't making this easy."

"It should be after you've had your b*ear* hands on me only moments ago." Blair licked her bottom lip and pulled it between her teeth.

Noah shook his head. "You think you're funny."

"*Bear* with me. I have more."

Noah's smile cracked. He sighed. "I'm a bear shifter."

Blair gasped. "I can *bear*ly believe it."

"Are you done?"

Her upper body jolted as she pinched her lips together, holding in her laugh. Noah moved closer and knelt on one knee in front of her. He gripped her chin between his fingers until she lost the laughter.

"And you're my fated mate." The rumble of the words was only low enough to reach between them. It didn't matter no one else was there to overhear. She took a deep breath, as if accepting what he'd said. Her eyes met his, and the heat of the animal inside him shone in his own.

"So I was right. This isn't real between us. It's all Fate."

"No. It's not all Fate. Fate wouldn't choose someone we wouldn't be attracted to on our own."

"Attraction is only physical. That says nothing about how spending a life together would work out."

Noah allowed himself to touch her more. He moved his hand from her chin and tucked her hair behind her ear, and followed the action with his gaze. "Do you think we're so incompatible? Because I don't."

"It's not as simple as that."

"It can be. But the only thing we can do is start."

"Start something that can't be undone." She shook her head.

"It's already too late, kitten." They'd touched. They'd kissed. They'd bonded in a way Noah felt in his core.

"I don't want that to be true."

Noah dropped his hand. "You don't want this." It explained why she was not only angry, but avoided him. With his next breath, he stood and put the distance between them again.

"I could say the same about you."

"What?"

"You haven't been able to form the words. You're scared too." She set her drink down on the end table with a calm neither of them had.

"Those two things aren't connected." A fear of a future with her hadn't ever crossed his mind. The words were difficult for a reason all their own. A lifetime secret that put so many people in danger. Not for a second did Noah believe Blair would betray shifters. If that had been her goal, she'd have done it already. She was smart enough to recognize the dangers the world had toward shifters.

"You're saying you want this?" No shock, just genuine curiosity heightened her tone.

"I want to touch you, hold you. I want to do so many dirty things to you, it makes my body ache."

Blair sighed. "That's all physical attraction. That isn't real."

"The fuck it isn't." Noah dropped his chin and dropped his control. He pulled her up from the couch. "You don't get to tell me what I feel isn't real." He took her mouth, moving his lips over hers with aggression until she opened for him.

His entire being calmed as she let him in. He slowed the kiss and stroked his tongue over hers. Their bodies melded together, although uneven with their size difference. Pulling her as close as possible, Noah let his arm band around her waist and a hand palm her ass.

Every piece of her was delicious to him. And that extended from her body to her mind. He saw the big heart she carried tucked in her pocket—not on her sleeve for others to see, but right where she could use it for those she cared about. He saw how she looked at everything with wondrous curiosity. And he saw her body as the matching puzzle piece to his own.

It was easy to understand the fight she had with Fate deciding for her. Time would show her that Fate wasn't the only one in the equation. Words might be a good idea at the moment to help explain that, but his bear stood on his hind legs and roared with triumph that his mate was in his arms.

"I'll give you sixty seconds to push me away, kitten." Noah's hips never stopped moving against her. She knew what was coming next. And it would be very real.

"Noah. It's getting harder to push you away." Blair's hands rested on his chest. He imagined those hands moving elsewhere.

"I know."

"You won't..." Her own gasps cut her off.

"Mate you?" He filled in her missing words and ran his teeth along her jaw. They were already sharp and ready to sink into his mate's flesh to seal the bond. "Not yet. Not this time." Not until she begged for it.

Not this time. Deep down, Blair knew this was it. There would be a next time, and a time after that, and after that. She may not want to admit it, but this felt real. Not trusting it didn't stop her from tilting her head back and giving him access.

"Noah?"

"You going to run off this time, kitten?" He set kisses behind her ear.

"No." She hated feeling like she didn't have a choice, but she wanted him. That was a choice on its own, she supposed.

"Good. I can't say I wouldn't chase after you." His hands slid to her hips, and he bunched her dress in his fists. Blair mimicked his actions and pulled at the hem of his shirt.

Noah abandoned her dress and pulled his shirt off. Seeing his bare chest made something in her core snap. Reaching for the waist of his jeans, she pulled.

"Slow down. I need your lips first. I haven't had enough of them."

She'd let him do whatever he wanted as long as he spoke like that. Gravely and low. A sound that played her body like an instrument. He didn't need more than his voice to make her weak in the knees. If she was strong enough, she'd admit that was part of why she avoided him. Just his voice in her dreams was enough.

Noah cupped her jaw and kissed her. The scruff on his face scraped against her, adding to the demand of his lips. Firm and full, they parted hers and he stroked his tongue over hers. Not a claiming, but measured movements told her she would be his soon. And she reveled in it. Oh, she shouldn't. She didn't want to give into Fate demanding this was her life.

His fists clenched in her dress again, and this time he didn't stop. In seconds, he bared her to him. Did she pick out the lace bra and panties with him in mind? Yes, she did.

He stepped back, and the look on his face didn't disappoint her. His eyes changed. Their shape and colour became sharper as he took her in.

"Damn."

Maybe it was a frivolous emotion, but knowing she affected him in that way made her feel powerful.

With a growl, he slid his hands down her sides. He bent as he lowered them to her thighs. Her stomach dropped as he gripped and lifted, bringing her legs around his waist. He stopped next to his front door on the way to the bedroom. "Last chance, Blair. Do you want to leave?"

"No. I don't." She rolled her hips.

"Fuck, kitten. This is going to be good."

Blair didn't bother looking at her surroundings as he kicked open one door before taking three more strides to toss her onto the bed. She stared as he reached for the fly of his jeans. Naked at the end of the bed, Noah fisted a hand around his cock and stroked.

She suddenly had tunnel vision, admiring the beauty of him. Large, graceful, and safe. Her fear of being his mate had nothing to do with Noah. Just the opposite. He called to her. The first time she'd been in Firebrook, and now.

She didn't have to come back here. She could have let this mystery go and avoided Noah. Was that Fate? Or her?

"Blair." Her name was sharp on his tongue and she snapped her gaze up to his. A sinful grin lifted his lips and narrowed his eyes. He let go of his cock and climbed onto the bed, straddling her legs. "It would be a shame to take this off of you." He traced the cups of the bra. She hesitated to think of it as a cup. It was sheer fabric that hugged her breasts. It wasn't something that provided any genuine support.

Back and forth, he ran his finger along the edge until he hooked the tips under the fabric and pulled it down. He bared her breast without taking off the bra. Repeating the same motion with the other one, he bent and ran his tongue around the first exposed nipple.

Her gasp pushed her breast closer to him.

She wanted more. Her body hummed and begged. The lace held her up like a feast. One that he murmured his enjoyment while he took. He sucked and nipped until she became restless beneath him. Then those wicked fingers dropped to the lace at her hips.

"Noah. You're going too slow."

He laughed. The damn bear laughed at her. "I'm going at the speed I want. I've dreamed of this too long to veer off my plans. There's so much of you to taste." His head moved between her breasts and those talented lips started kissing their way down her torso.

As he scooted his body down, his lips lined up with her clit. His hot breath penetrated the lace. She didn't dare move. He could stop if she moved.

He peeled the lace down. With her legs pinned together under him, they only went down far enough to expose the vertex he teased with the air from his panting breath. He was as aroused as she.

Whimpers escaped, shaky and raw, when Noah flicked his tongue over her clit. "That sounds lovely, kitten." He repeated the motion and kept working the sensitive button until each sound she made rolled into the next. Soon, she didn't recognize the low keening from her throat.

Noah adjusted himself so he was between her legs rather than straddling. Lifting her feet to his chest, he peeled the panties away.

"Too slow, Noah," she complained.

He chuckled. "You need to come first. Maybe twice. I've wanted inside you for so long, I won't last."

If she had half her senses, she'd tease him, but she'd rather he didn't have a reason to drag this out any longer than he already was.

Noah lowered himself and grinned up at her. His mouth hovered over her clit and she felt the barest of touches at her opening. "Purr for me, kitten." He thrust two fingers inside her and latched onto her clit to suck hard.

She cried out and bucked her hips. Noah followed before banding his free arm over her waist.

He worked her hard and fast. Her climax rose like a fierce wind to crash against a cliff and spin back around to whip her. She held her breath, reaching for the peak of pleasure. Noah curled his fingers, and she fell. Hard waves wracked her body and Noah slowed his pace to settle the climax.

"You make such sweet sounds." He murmured against her, then slid his fingers into his mouth.

Nothing that came out of her was something she'd describe as sweet. She hadn't recognized herself. And if he wasn't looking at her with awe, she wouldn't believe him.

"Fuck, Blair. I can't wait." Noah moved up her body, stole her lips, and pushed into her. Blair let the sensations overwhelm her, knowing she'd choose this moment. Fate or no Fate.

Noah snaked his hand to the back of Blair's neck. He held her in place while he found his rhythm. He'd expected her to bolt the moment he had a hold on her dress.

Blair's hips bucked beneath his, meeting every thrust he made. More than the sensations of sex scraped down his spine. Something close to the feeling of home. Of something divine and right washed through him. It scared him to tell her that. That screamed of Fate poking her nose in, but Noah wasn't so sure. This felt like it was part of him. That it was an extension of him.

Now that he admitted his truth to her, a weight had lifted. He doubted it was the end of his struggles.

He was getting close, and it was going to be explosive. He wanted her to get the most out of this, not having any reason to doubt.

"Come, kitten."

"I'm not there, yet. So close." She threw her head back. There was no way she understood the temptation that caused him. Her smooth column called to him. His teeth, already sharp, lengthened. Magic whispered in his ear. *Mate.* His bear crowed with victory. Noah had to put a stop to it.

Pulling free, he gripped her hips to flip her. She let out a growl of her own, but he ignored it and shoved back in from behind. The sound she made after that was somewhere between a gasp and a sigh.

With his hands gripping her ass hard enough to leave fingertip bruises, he buried himself in her soft heat over and over. Harder and harder.

"What do you need, kitten?"

"I don't know." She was breathy and his ears were ringing enough she sounded lost in the room.

"Touch yourself. Come with me." He couldn't hold back much longer, but he needed more from her. Needed to give her more.

She slid a hand beneath her and reached down. Her walls clamped around him the moment her fingers made contact.

Running a hand up her spine, he fisted her hair.

"Noah!" She cried out his name and her climax followed the sound. The moment her core squeezed him, he exploded. He spilled into her body and his teeth clamped onto his tongue rather than bending forward to sink into her neck.

He held her hips against him until the spasms of his orgasm settled. As soon as he let her go, she slid forward onto the bed. Breaths still sawed in and out of his chest as he walked to the bathroom to get a cloth.

Blair stirred as he cleaned her up. Biting her lip, she tracked him as he took the cloth back to the bathroom. When he returned, she rolled to her back. Noah climbed over her to settle on her other side. She stiffened as he pulled her toward him.

"Don't do that, Blair."

"Do what?"

"Don't go back and forth. There's nothing wrong with what we did. We both had more than enough chances to back out."

She sighed. "You're right. I don't mean to seem like I regret it. I don't. It's hard to see the difference between Fate and us."

"It's not as difficult as you're making it out to be." Noah understood that now. Fate put them together, said they're meant to be, but the emotions they have for each other are their own. "Give it time, Blair. But don't push away."

"I'll try."

"Stay the night?"

She didn't answer him right away, but she snuggled closer against him and ran her hand over his chest. "I'm going to go. But not yet." She pressed her lips to his shoulder.

Noah took what he could get, not arguing that leaving now was pushing him away, but she wasn't leaving Firebrook.

"Why was it so hard for you to tell me?"

Running his fingers up and down her arm, he turned his head to breathe in her scent. "It's been a lifelong secret. The safety of shifters depends on it staying secret. You already knowing didn't make a difference to my stubborn head. It felt wrong to say the words aloud to someone who wasn't family."

Blair pushed off his chest and looked down at him. Narrowed eyes studied his face. "Bullshit."

Noah blinked back at her in shock.

"I mean, I'm sure that's true. I don't think you're lying, but there was more to it than that. Something else made those words difficult to say."

Noah didn't like what filled his chest. It would have been so much easier if she'd come out and asked him.

"It's one thing for you to leave me when I can pretend you don't know, but once it's out there, I can't imagine the pain of you leaving."

The concentration she had in her eyes vanished and she paled. Panic squeezed his heart. That look was a peek into her thoughts on the future. It was too soon to jump to conclusions. Noah ignored the panic and ran his knuckle down her cheek. It more important now to build the connection and trust between them.

Her tongue ran along her lips before she leaned down to kiss him. It was a sweet exploration that heated the longer she held him under her. He ran his hands up her body, but she wouldn't let him pull her down.

"I'll see you Friday." Her face cleared and she let her lips lift into a mischievous grin.

If she'd said any other type of goodbye, he'd have rolled her back on the mattress fast enough to knock the wind out of both of them. But if she still planned to climb with him, then he hadn't lost her. Not yet. He'd have to keep it that way.

She slid from the bed and fixed her bra that still held her breasts out. Frowning at the floor, she spun. Noah bit back his laugh. She couldn't find her panties and her dress was in the living room.

"Need help, kitten?"

"No." She walked to the other side of the bed.

"Too bad." Noah wouldn't let her go back to her cabin alone, anyway. Not at this hour. It may not be that late, but it was getting dark. He found her panties before she did and held them out to her on his finger. He pulled his jeans on and followed her to the living room. She found her dress and had it on by the time he found his shirt.

"Why are you getting dressed?" She crossed her arms.

"I'm taking you home." That was obvious, in his opinion.

"I brought my car."

"Then I'll come for the drive." Did she think he wouldn't see her home? Then again, she didn't know he'd followed her home every night he'd seen her. He may not have knocked on the door or made himself known, but he wasn't capable of letting her go home alone.

"And how will you get back here?"

"Two feet. Or four paws." He shrugged and stopped her before she argued any more. "Let's go, kitten. I'll even let you drive." The look she threw him was worth the tease.

Noah had his mate close. He wouldn't do anything to jeopardize their future. She wouldn't regret choosing him. He just had to make it clear this was their decision and not Fate's. Blair wouldn't settle for anything less.

Chapter Five

After a lively breakfast with Poppy, Dakota, and Bonnie at the bakery where she avoided every mention of Noah, Blair took a second coffee to go and went straight to the library. She'd stalked up and down Brenton Road the day before while thinking about Noah and hadn't come up with any reason Scott and Luca would be on this street.

She roamed the library, admiring the welcoming feel they'd created for the small community. Plush chairs around fireplaces created two large reading corners. Partitioned desks gave students privacy for studying. The entire environment rivaled a big city library with all the amenities. Blair would choose this place over those any day.

They had every genre available and their non-fiction section spanned several shelves. But the section that made her frown was the one labeled archives. Not that archives were odd, but Scott and Luca had never been readers and she doubted they'd taken up the hobby while plotting murder. But archives held information.

Making her way back to the front desk, she smiled at the librarian waiting there.

"Hello." Blair kept her voice hushed.

"Hi there. What can I help you with?"

Blair twisted her smile. "I'm looking for information on some people that may have come in here."

The librarian frowned, cautious of what Blair was about to say.

"Do you remember the events that happened here in June?"

"Yes." She voiced the word with the inflection of a question.

"The two men. Were they ever in here?"

"Oh." She blinked as if that hadn't been what she expected Blair to ask. "Yes. Twice."

"What were they looking for? Did they check anything out of the library?"

"They didn't. They searched through the archive section for almost two hours and left looking angry." She shook her head. "No, not quite angry. Frustrated. They checked the event schedule before they left. The next time they came back, they only hovered while classes took place."

"What classes?"

"I'm sorry. I can't remember. We have so many. But I can give you a copy of our summer schedule if that would help?"

"Please. Thank you."

The librarian tapped on the keyboard in front of her. A few minutes later, the sound of an old printer creaked beneath her. She reached down and pulled up a calendar printed on a single sheet of paper. "Here are the programs from this past June. Some of them are still ongoing, but others only last a few weeks."

"Which ones are shorter?"

"It's colour coded. Programs in blue run all year long. The orange ones are summer only. And pink are the short-term classes."

"This is very helpful. Thank you so much." Blair pulled out a card and passed it to her. "If you think of anything else, will you please call me?"

"Absolutely."

"Thank you. Have a great day."

"You, too." The librarian called back to her and watched Blair leave. It didn't give her any answers, but she had a lead of some sort.

In her car, she looked over the program schedule. Most of the summer programs catered to children. Summer camps, story time, story creation, and arts and crafts days. The adult programs that ran all year had a book club or two, paint nights, and a knitting group. Nothing that struck a cord or set an antenna high.

Leaning over the passenger seat of her car, Blair looked out the window at the building. Firebrook had proved low tech, but they must have security cameras. The library had one.

She'd looked for them inside, but they only covered entrances and exits. If she convinced someone to show her the footage, she could at least determine when Scott and Luca had been at the library and narrow down which one of these programs had caught their attention.

Across the street was the police station. They may not be as forthcoming with information as the public who loved to talk. That route had to wait.

The other end of the street had the town's only school. The building itself looked new and large, with different wings, housing everyone from kindergarten to high school. A building connected to the police station with its own entrance. The sign read *Town Hall - Municipality of Firebrook*. Above it hung an older looking sign that only had the words *Town Hall* etched on it. This place loved its charm. It was something Blair noticed on many buildings—a new sign below the older, traditional or historic one.

All the buildings on this street were rooted in Firebrook, the place, and the people. So had Scott and Luca been trying to find a place or a person? Or information? Not expecting to get far, Blair hopped out of her car and jogged across the street to the Town Hall.

A woman that looked eerily like the librarian sat behind a large desk in the centre of an empty lobby. Several doors circled the main level and stairs behind the desk led to another floor.

"Good morning. Can I help you?" The woman spoke cheerfully enough it echoed.

"I hope so. I have a question I was hoping you'd be able to answer."

"I'll certainly try." She readied her hands at her computer and tilted her head back to look up at Blair.

"I'm trying to find some answers. Do you remember the events that happened here in June?" It wouldn't be much longer and Blair wouldn't have to ask that anymore. Word would spread that she was out asking questions, and the locals would either seek her out or avoid her.

"Everyone does." She tilted her head with a don't-you-know-it look.

"Did they ever come in here?"

"The men who killed their friend and kidnapped Poppy?"

Blair nodded.

"They did." She lowered her tone as if she didn't want someone to overhear.

"What were they looking for?"

"They didn't say, only asked to see resident records. They wouldn't say what residents or what about them. I turned them away. It wasn't information I could give them, anyway." Her eyes rolled behind her glasses as if that was obvious.

"Is that information stored in this building? Maybe the library or the police station next door?" Would there be information on residents in the library archives? Maybe nothing direct, but the archives held things like local newspapers.

"It is." She confirmed with a nod.

"Thank you. I appreciate you telling me."

"Can I ask why you want to know?" She leaned forward on her desk and frowned.

"I'm a friend of Poppy's. I was here in June as well. I just want to know why." Telling people she was an investigative journalist didn't always go well. This wasn't only a story that needed an ending, but it was personal.

"Oh, you're one of the girls they kidnapped with Poppy." The woman's eyes widened and her hand landed on her chest.

Blair nodded and gave a sad smile.

"Well, I understand wanting answers. I'm sorry I couldn't be more help. But anything more than that, I couldn't tell you, anyway."

"I understand. Thank you so much." Blair left. Person, place, or information. But whichever it was, it had to do with someone in Firebrook.

Noah couldn't get Blair's scent or taste out of his senses. His day had turned into a blur as he left *Rockhard* and drove straight to Blair's cabin. Joy and calm spread through his chest as he saw her car parked. The little car he'd barely fit in when they drove back here the night before. He didn't plan on climbing into the teeny tiny box again.

He knocked and listened to her light feet cross the small cabin. She opened the door and the smile on her face was slow to spread—like watching a memory play out. The longer she looked at him, the bigger the smile got.

"Hi, kitten."

"Hi." She licked her lips. Noah thought the motion was unconsciously done. "I didn't know you were coming by."

"I didn't either."

Blair stepped back and let him in. It wasn't the first time he'd been in the smallest of his cousins' cabins, but he looked around with fresh eyes, wondering how the hell Caiden had lived in this one for as long as he had. Noah cringed at the thought of trying to fit himself in here for anything more than a few hours. Or overnight, as he hoped he would with Blair.

He didn't want to go home. At least not alone.

The tension grew, like a bubble of air that formed between them. Small to start, shiny and fragile as it widened. But Blair shook her head and popped the entire thing with a high-pitched tone.

"I haven't eaten."

"Neither have I." Food wasn't on his mind.

"I have a frozen pizza." She pointed to the stove where an unopened box sat.

"How about we order in pizza?"

"Frozen pizza isn't good enough for you?" She crossed her arms over her chest and cocked her hip. More than once he'd had a dream about her standing that way, telling him off and then kissing her to shut her up.

"Frozen is fine. But it's not enough." He'd eat two of those things on his own.

"You eat that much?" She looked skeptical.

"Yes."

"You didn't last night." He'd eaten the same amount as her.

"I was preoccupied." With secrets that had needed to be told and a mate that needed to be claimed.

"Oh, so it's all out of the way and now you can eat. Gee, thanks."

Noah reached forward and circled her waist with his hands. One quick pull and she landed against his chest and he kissed her. He kissed her with all the memories of last night and all the promises to come.

When he pulled back, Blair looked up at him with something close to stunned until she blinked it away.

"That isn't at all the case. I'll still be hungry after we recreate last night."

She ran her hands up his chest and sighed. Not the kind he'd hoped for, but the one that said wait a minute. "Maybe that isn't a good idea."

"Why wouldn't it be?"

"Let the first night finish settling." She slipped her hand in his pocket and pulled out his phone while she pushed away from him. "Order your pizza."

Turning away, she put the frozen one back in the small freezer.

He clenched his teeth to hold back his disappointment while he dialed *Bobby's Pizza Pub*. Blair wanted the distance. But at least she hadn't pushed him out the door, telling him to leave her alone. Noah had no reason to be upset yet. If she needed time, he'd give it to her, just not alone.

Bobby's son answered and took his order.

"Can you deliver to the small cabin at Bearbrook?"

"Uh, sure."

"Thanks."

The kid hung up.

"It will be here soon." Noah refrained from crossing the space to where she leaned against the counter.

Blair chewed her lip and stared at everything but him. Those wheels of hers never stopped working.

"Blair?" He wanted her to share.

"Why is this awkward?" She gave a half laugh and still wouldn't meet his gaze.

"It's not." At least it wasn't for him, and he wasn't sure why it would be for her.

"Not for you. I don't know what to do with you in my space." Her hands let go of the counter and she crossed her arms like a barrier.

"I can help with that." He dropped his tone and let a grin share his thoughts. It was too easy, and exactly what he wanted to do.

"Not like that." She glared. "Where do we go from here?"

"Wherever we want. Fate has done her job. The rest is up to us."

"Fate has done her job?" Offense filled each word. This was what he'd have trouble getting her to understand. It was his own assessment, with no proof, but one that other shifters seemed to share.

"Tell me something, kitten." Noah couldn't stay out of her reach for this. "How did you feel last night?"

"You were there." She blushed through her sarcasm and wasn't that the sweetest thing to see? Blair was full of fire and he doubted she blushed often.

"Yes. I know how you felt physically. But that isn't what I'm talking about." He slid his hands over her hips. "Close your eyes."

"I don't want to." She shook her head and her body trembled. Those eyes looked up at him, focusing on his face, but not his eyes.

"Do it, kitten. Please."

She closed her eyes; her lashes resting on her still flushed cheeks. Noah leaned in, but didn't touch her with anything other than his hands. He drew circles on her hips with his thumbs, timing them to her breaths.

"I know what your physical reaction is. I can see it. I feel the same. And I can smell it. I want to know what else you feel and where is it coming from?"

"I can't separate it." It was the first time Noah had ever heard her sound small.

"Yes, you can." He lifted one hand off her hip and set it against her chest. "When you separate it, you'll see Fate isn't here."

Her eyes snapped open, and she locked them onto his. Gentle hands pushed him away. She could have shoved, but she didn't. The motion put distance between them. "Do you want something to drink?"

"Sure." Noah stomped on his disappointment. She didn't deserve it.

Blair pulled iced tea from the fridge and poured two glasses.

"What did you do today?" He kept his tone conversational, so she didn't think he was prying as she had before.

"I had breakfast with friends. Then I checked out the library." She sipped at her glass and moved to the couch, sinking gracefully down onto it. Noah joined her, trying not to read into the slight increase in her heart rate.

"Oh? Find anything interesting?"

"Yes, very interesting." And just like that, her face switched to the one she had when asking too many questions. The look that made his endearment for her meaningful.

"Kitten?" Noah leaned back against the couch, hoping she'd open up to him on her own.

"Hmm?" She looked at him.

"What were you looking for at the library?"

"What does anyone look for at a library?" She attempted a *well-duh* look, but it didn't land with him. She left something out.

"Did you know shifters have an exceptional sense of smell?"

"Yes." She frowned.

"We can sense subtle shifts in people when they feel different things while speaking. Like when they're excited, sad, stressed, lying." He tried not to grit his teeth at divulging more information about shifters. It was a little easier since last night, but a hard habit to break, even for his mate.

"That's fascinating." She brought one knee up on the couch and faced him, her attention divided between what he said and what she hid.

"Blair." He hadn't intended the warning to come out with a growl. And his damn mate only smiled back at him.

"Noah." She returned with extra sweetness.

He set his glass down before he broke it in his grip. Taking hers from her hand, he set it next to his. Then, in one swift motion, Noah grabbed her hips and pulled her on top of him. Her squeal was oddly satisfying. With her straddling him, he held her in place even when she tried to push off. Her eyes widened when she realized he could overpower her with only a hold on her hips.

He'd hold her against him for as long as it took to convince her not to follow the dangerous path she was on.

B lair gripped Noah's shoulders. His hold was almost bruising and she couldn't free herself.

"What were you looking for at the library, Blair?" All subtle conversation vanished. Noah wanted the answers she'd avoided giving him.

"Not your business." That might not be the wisest response, but she didn't want him to stop her from finding out what Scott and Luca had been doing here in June.

"Everything about you is my business now."

"Is that so?" The asshole. "Is that how it works in your world? You fucked me so now you get to know everything about me?"

His lip curled up. The scruff on his face made the look more sexy than scary. "That isn't what we did last night. Don't debase what's between us."

Blair swallowed. For a man so closed off and grumpy, Noah felt big. Not his size, his emotions, his feelings toward her. It was the first sign she'd gotten of something bigger than Fate.

When he'd held his hand against her chest and asked her to separate from the physical reaction, she'd refused. Sure, she'd closed her eyes and wanted to try, but the minute something else took hold, it choked her.

The likelihood of Fate getting it right every single time was unrealistic. Fate created horrible things in this world—She wasn't responsible for only the good. Poppy and Wyatt worked. So did Bonnie and Easton, and Maggie and Caiden. But surely they were the minority.

They'd gotten lucky that Fate had chosen right for them. Or Fate still worked her magic. Blair didn't deal with blind faith.

But faith didn't stare back at her through Noah. And she didn't think it was Fate either.

"I didn't mean to do that." Last night had meant something to her and had to him.

"I didn't just fuck you." His eyes glowed, but he blinked it away. Blair ignored the glimpse of his bear. For now.

"I know. But what happened last night between us doesn't automatically give you the right to know everything about me." Blair let go of some of her anger after seeing how her words had hurt him.

"What you're doing is dangerous."

Blair shrugged. She shouldn't tell him it wasn't the worst situation she'd been in.

"Then include me."

"What?"

"Don't go anywhere or do anything without telling me first."

"Um, no. I will not be accountable to you for everything I do. This is my job."

"So work asked you to find this story?" His head tilted in a way that said he didn't think that was true.

"No," she said through clenched teeth. Apparently, lying was useless.

"I don't care if you think it's Fate or me, but I care about you and I couldn't live with myself if you got hurt, especially when I'm close enough to help." He loosened his grip enough to change it. He moved his hands up to her waist, under her shirt. His touch was warm, but the heat of passion between them was held at bay.

She sighed. Fighting him wasn't doing her any good. "Fine. I'm trying to find out what Scott and Luca were doing here. Firebrook is the connection. Not Poppy or the bar she used to work at. They were looking for something or someone here in Firebrook."

"And what's your plan if they find out you're here chasing their trail? If you're right, why wouldn't they come back?"

"If they come back, I'll have some fresh tracks to follow." It would make this that much easier.

Noah's hand tightened again, and his chest rumbled.

"Everything will be fine."

"What do you think they would have done with you if we hadn't caught them after they'd kidnapped you and your friends?" Noah and his brother had gone with Wyatt to rescue them from the trunk of the car.

"I don't know." Blair cleared her throat and looked away.

Rough fingers gripped her chin and turned her face back to him. "Blair..." He started, but she cut him off.

"No. Don't ask me to stop because I won't."

A knock on the door startled her enough to jolt her body on his lap. "Pizza."

He set her back on the couch beside him. He stalked to the door and chatted with the delivery guy, pulling his wallet out of his back pocket.

Blair took several deep breaths while he focused on someone else for the next few seconds. He cared. He cared a lot. And Blair didn't know what to do with that information.

Chapter Six

B lair wouldn't let him spend the night. They finished eating, and
Noah put the two leftover slices in the fridge for her.

"How about I sleep on the couch?" Noah pulled her against him
with his arms around her waist.

"No."

He didn't like the idea of leaving her alone, knowing who she was
chasing. The bastards had escaped months ago, and no one had seen
them since, but if Blair was right and they had a reason for coming to
Firebrook, then they'd be back. They hadn't hesitated to take Blair
last time. They'd do worse this time.

"I think slow is better." She didn't realize he wanted to stay to watch
over her. And he wasn't about to correct her, which meant suggesting
he sleep in his truck wasn't a good idea.

With a small sigh, he bent his head and kissed her. Slowly, just as
she'd requested. He played with her, taking things a little further with
every slide of his tongue. Noah tried to keep his hands still, but he
wasn't successful. One hand fisted her shirt, and the other slid to the
back of her neck and into her hair.

The sound she made vibrated against his mouth and he returned
it with a growl. He backed her to the small counter and banded his
arm around her waist. With a quick lift, she sat on the counter and he
stood between her legs. Their lips never broke contact.

Noah settled against her and took the kiss deeper, feeding her the strength of the bond between them. He'd never tell her Fate hadn't been at play, but She wasn't part of this anymore. Not since June. When Noah had called her over and over after she'd left, it was because he wanted to hear her voice. He wanted to see her. Fate sewed that connected thread, but the rest was up to them.

He brought her to the end of the counter so their centres touched. He was hard and ready, and the scent of her arousal was a potent aphrodisiac. But Noah kept things at only a kiss unless she asked for more.

The passion seemed to take root and Blair bowed her back so she pressed her breasts to his chest. Her hands delved into his hair and pulled. She'd lost herself in this as much as he.

Panting, she turned her head away and his lips moved to her neck. "Noah?"

"Yeah, kitten?" he murmured against her skin.

"You need to go." Her hands pulled him closer.

"Need? I need something and it isn't leaving. Let me make you come, kitten. Then I'll leave." It wouldn't be enough and would only make this more painful for him later, but he wanted to give her something. This didn't need to be hard for her.

"You want... What?" She leaned back and pulled his head away from her neck.

"Let me make you come." He moved his hands to the button of her jeans and waited.

One breath. Two. A third and she nodded.

He undid her jeans and pulled her from the counter to push them down her legs. Once they hung around her ankles, he lifted her back in place and tore the jeans from her feet.

One more kiss that he ended with a nip, then he dropped to one knee and spread her legs. "Lean back." He gripped her hips, tilting them toward him and setting her on the edge.

Noah inhaled and closed his eyes. Her sweet and spicy scent was almost enough to make him come. He craved her taste. Needed it like he needed to breathe.

Running his cheek along the inside of her thigh, he moved closer until his nose nuzzled her soft flesh.

"Noah." His name came out like a strangled whine.

He chuckled and flicked his tongue over her clit. She trembled from that touch alone, and Noah gave her no mercy after that. He worked her clit until she tried to pull away. Holding her tight with one hand, he used the other to insert two fingers.

He could draw this out, make it slow, but he was having trouble keeping his control. If he didn't leave soon, he wouldn't be. He curled his fingers and latched onto her clit with ferocity. Her hand slammed back against the cupboards and she cried out while rocking her hips against his face. He didn't stop, and he didn't slow, extending her climax. When her cries turned into whimpers, he released her.

Noah stood and held her until her breathing returned and some of her muscles tensed. She lifted her head and her lips parted, but before she spoke, Noah cut her off with a kiss. He didn't want to say anything, and he didn't want to hear her kick him out.

Ensuring she was steady, he set her on her feet. With a final kiss to her forehead, he turned and left.

He turned his truck into a parking spot outside the main lodge instead of driving home. If he went home, the only thing he'd be doing was jacking off in the shower and making himself more miserable. He stalked past all the cabins, veering around the back of Blair's, and went straight for the woods.

Stashing his clothes in the bushes, he pulled on the magic. Warmth spread through his body as the wind circled him. He welcomed the ache of joints popping and bones changing as it took away from the desire still rolling through him.

Seconds passed, and he landed on the ground with four paws and covered in fur, a barrier from the chill. Stretching, he let himself run off some energy before returning to the edge of the trees.

He'd spend the night watching over Blair's cabin. He couldn't stop her from chasing Scott and Luca's trail, but he wouldn't let her be alone if he could help it. The long days away from her at work wouldn't help. And her wanting to take things slow made it that much harder.

Noah might enjoy the time with her, to coax her into mating, if she weren't putting herself in danger.

Her back creaked as Blair got out of bed. She swore she'd aged a decade overnight. The tick of every minute she didn't sleep felt like a month. Noah's attempt at giving her pleasure before leaving backfired. Heat pulsed under her skin, forcing her to kick the blankets from her body all night. The hot flashes left her drenched in sweat.

Normal attraction didn't cause uncontrollable arousal, aches, sleeplessness, and hot flashes. Fate and her fucking notions disturbed her body chemistry to force her to go to him. And Noah tried to claim this was real.

Blair shook her head as she stretched her back for the umpteenth time after closing the door behind her. She paused on the steps. Warmth trickled over the back of her neck. She'd had the same feeling throughout the night, but stronger. Looking around, the lane was empty.

Shaking it off, Blair got in her car and headed out for her morning jolt of coffee before heading back to the library.

A familiar truck sat parked at the main lodge. He was here. She stopped in the middle of the lane, chewing on the inside of her lip.

She wanted to ignore him and get to work. It wasn't his business what she did. Blair wouldn't fault anyone for their concern of others, but neither would she stop living her life or doing what she loved. And she loved her job.

But the ache in her chest urged her to go inside and talk to him. He needed to understand, some things she'd never let go. And since he left the night before, things felt unresolved—hovering in limbo with her toes stretched toward the ground.

A quick good morning and plans to meet for lunch. In public. She could manage that.

She parked her car next to his truck and went inside. Maggie sat on a stool behind the front counter.

"Good morning, Blair." The quiet redhead always had the most welcoming smile. She was a calming beauty.

"Good morning." Blair spared Maggie a smile, then looked around, spinning in a circle.

"What are you looking for?" Maggie turned her head around the room as if the answer would be obvious once she spotted it.

"Noah." Blair stretched up to look behind Maggie into the small kitchen area.

"He isn't here."

"His truck is out front." She hitched her thumb over her shoulder and kept turning her head.

"Has been all night. No one has seen him." Maggie shook her head.

All night. Noah never went home. "Where does a bear shifter go when he doesn't go home and no one can find him?"

Maggie pursed her lips. She knew. She was married to one. The fated mate of Noah's cousin. "Check the woods behind your cabin." Not quite a whisper, but secrecy shrouded Maggie's tone.

"Thanks." Blair tried hard not to growl or to stomp her feet as she left the lodge and got back in her car. But she did hit the gas pedal a little too hard, kicking up gravel as she sped back up to her cabin. Slamming her car door, she stormed into the trees.

She slowed as she stepped over brush and debris rather than taking the walking trail. A bear who didn't want to be seen wouldn't be on a walking trail. But he wouldn't be far, either. Turning, she saw most of the trees block her car and cabin.

"I know you're here!"

She winced when silence responded. Sure, make her the crazy person yelling into the woods.

"Stop hiding!"

Debris crunched in the distance. Her breath caught despite knowing it was only Noah. But the likelihood that it was Noah as a bear had only just occurred to her.

Another crunch.

Blair spun, searching for him. No one was near. The trees held a peaceful calm, with only the sounds of birds and an approaching grizzly bear.

The next few steps were louder and a puff of air from a large nose came through loud and clear. Turning again, Blair saw the bear ten yards ahead of her, his head visible between trees.

Oh, he was big. A grizzly wasn't a small animal, but as a shifter, the size alone set another level of terror. But this wasn't just a bear. This was Noah.

His eyes, while a different shape, still held his heart. It felt weird to think like that, but she had no other way to explain what she saw there.

"You..." She cleared her throat. "You didn't go home."

Noah lumbered closer, then he closed his eyes and bowed his head. A visible wind swirled around him and warmth filled the space. His fur receded and his body changed. Blair didn't want to turn away, but she shielded her ears against the sound of bones popping and grinding. It sounded painful, but seconds later, Noah stood in front of her, naked and not an ounce of pain in his features.

"You didn't go home." She didn't need the repetition except to refocus herself from seeing him in his naked glory.

"No."

"No?" Blair blinked and forced her gaze up. "Why not?"

He didn't answer. Didn't move. He stood like a rigid, flawless statue, except this statue had a hard on he ignored.

"I asked you to leave. I wanted space to take things slow. Why did you stay here in the woods?"

"I left, and I gave you space. You didn't know I was here."

"But you were here!"

"Blair..." he started, but stopped with a harsh sigh.

"I want to know things will work out on their own. That isn't too much to ask. You should have gone home."

"I couldn't go home."

"And you call this real? If this was real, Fate would have allowed you to go home. Fate would give us the space and trust."

"That's not why I stayed. This is all very real, kitten." Noah stalked closer, his bare feet easily walking over leaves and twigs.

"Then why..." It hit her. "You're watching over me."

"I can't let anything happen to you."

Blair deflated. It wasn't fair to be upset with someone who only cared. But that didn't change the fact she wanted the space, the physical distance put between them every single day as a test for Fate and this bond that he claimed was real.

"Blair." Her name came out like a growl, and his fingers reached for her face. The barest of touches was all it took for her body to light on fire.

She gasped and stepped back. "No. It doesn't matter what I'm doing or why I'm in Firebrook. That isn't your business. I'm not in any danger by asking the locals what they know. It's just questions. Distance, Noah. I want the physical distance and a chance to be sure everything running through me is my own." Unlike how she'd felt all night. How could she be sure now that hadn't been caused by him being so close?

"Questions can cause a lot of trouble if they don't want you to know something." The muscles at the base of his neck grew. "You aren't taking this seriously."

"I take my job very seriously." He didn't have the right to accuse her of carelessness. "It's not as if they caught me searching their house and locked me in their basement before setting the house on fire." She blurted the story rather than biting her tongue.

Not only his neck and shoulder grew, but his entire body thickened and tensed. "What was that, kitten?"

H is body felt as if his insides formed into rock. "What was that, kitten?"

"Hypothetically, Noah."

But it wasn't. The moment the words finished falling from her lips, her blood pumped harder. It drummed in his ears. Her eyes dilated with fear. And her scent tinged ever so slightly with citrus. Not her natural scent, but the one he recognized when she lied.

"I'm only making a point. This isn't dangerous."

"Bullshit." He had to hold her. Without his hands on her, he had no way to stop her. "That was a lie."

"Right. It was a hypothetical story." The citrus scent grew stronger and her heart beat faster.

"That story was true." Noah gripped her waist and pulled her against him. Something inside him calmed. Contact meant safe. She was safe as long as he could hold her.

Blair set her hands on his forearms and squeezed. "It isn't your business. I asked for space. I can take care of myself."

"If you could take care of yourself, you never would have been locked in a basement, locked in the trunk of a car, or chasing after murderers with an unknown motive."

"I also wouldn't be here if I couldn't take care of myself." She pushed away from him. "Make a choice, Noah. I can't trust what is between us unless I know it is *us* controlling it. Give me space."

Give her time to trust Fate's choice and leave her vulnerable, or watch over her and possibly lose her. Either decision could mean he'd lose her. "You're asking too much."

She stumbled back a few steps. "I'm asking too much?"

That hadn't been the smartest thing he'd said in his lifetime, but he wouldn't take it back. No matter how he attacked this, all he heard was her asking him to let her go. Now that he'd opened up.

Blair pointed at him, her finger lining up with his face. "Don't follow me." She turned and ran, getting back in her car to drive off.

Noah didn't have a choice. He had to hope he was near if anything happened. He'd have to hope she never saw him when he followed her. For now, he needed to go to work. He needed the distraction.

He took the time to go home and shower before going in, arriving an hour late. Tavis had everything under control, as they didn't have any scheduled climbs for when they opened, but the first would arrive soon.

"Cutting it a little close."

"I'll be cutting it close for the next little while."

"Things didn't go so well with Blair?" Tavis inhaled. A shower wouldn't erase all of her scent, or his manic state. "Or they did go well?"

"Both. She wants space and doesn't trust Fate."

"I can't blame her for that."

"No. I can't either, but that doesn't make it easy. I'm trying to make her understand."

"We didn't understand until not so long ago. Give her the space."

Noah held his brother's gaze.

"What is it?" Tavis tilted his head.

"She's tracking clues from the murder in June." Maybe Noah shouldn't let that out, but if there was anyone he trusted most, it was his brother.

"And you're letting her?" He almost yelled.

Laughter built in his chest, but his panic still had a tight grip. As if Blair needed permission from anyone. She sure as hell wasn't looking to him for it. "You try to stop her."

"She isn't my mate." Being her mate wasn't enough.

"Yours will come." They all would, and it seemed sooner rather than later if the past year had any indication.

Tavis huffed, letting the conversation drop now that it had turned on him. "The group coming in has four, two couples. Easy enough to split." He sat on the stool behind the computer and put himself to work. Noah went outside to sort through gear.

Not that he needed to. The two of them were disgustingly organized with their business. They always put the gear back a certain way to ensure they'd have easy and quick access for whatever situation. Different sizes were available for group lessons or individual lessons, their own personal gear, and gear used for emergencies for search and rescue.

Noah was only sifting through it all when the breeze blew in a scent strong enough to bring him to his knees. He gripped the edge of the bin to keep himself standing as Tavis brought back the two couples. Noah smiled, but he knew it didn't quite reach his eyes. Blair's scent still wrapped sharp tendrils around his lungs. He was stuck here while she was in search of danger. Danger she didn't need to chase.

Curious kitten that couldn't let things go. Except him. She had no problem pushing him away.

Thankfully, Tavis did most of the talking while Noah pulled out the gear for each person and set it at their feet. His brother must have sensed his preoccupation because he checked every pile himself. Noah needed to get his head straight.

"Looking good, everyone. We're just going to grab some water and we'll be right back." Noah clasped his hand on his brother's shoulder and pulled him back inside.

"We have water out there." Tavis stated the obvious, but waited for whatever Noah needed.

"Punch me."

"What?" A grin spread over his face.

"You heard me and it would be great if you didn't make me repeat it. I'm not concentrating. And if I can't concentrate, I shouldn't be out there with you."

"You're right. But just to be clear. You want me to do what?" Tavis already set his foot back and made a fist. As soon as Noah let the words loose, he'd hit him.

Noah closed his eyes and said, "Punch me." His head whipped sideways with the force and pain exploded in his jaw.

"That was fun. Anytime you need to be set straight, I'm here for you, man."

"Yeah." Noah rubbed his jaw. "Thanks." But the pain distracted him from Blair's scent and the memory of her taste long enough for him to get through the first climbing lesson. The next one on the schedule might be a different story.

* * *

Chapter Seven

*I*t's okay for him to care. It's nice that he cares. He did his best to give me space. Saying those over and over only helped Blair breathe easier. They didn't make a difference because she could still feel him. His leaving the night before surprised her, but she'd trusted that he left. Now, as she walked out of Bella's Bakery, she felt like she was being watched.

His reason, though a sweet one, worked for a normal situation. But the story she chased wasn't even close to dangerous. Yet. She'd been around enough to experience sudden changes, but at this moment, Blair was as safe as she could be.

The heat of his eyes on her back made her whirl around as she walked north toward the library again. Most of the programs for the summer were still ongoing and Blair intended to check them out. All of them. Something would stand out.

The librarian at the front remembered her instantly and let her in the back of the pottery class already ongoing. Blair slipped in unnoticed and sat on a stool in the corner.

The instructor was in her mid twenties with messy hair piled high on her head. Blotches of clay stuck to her arms and face, and paint of multiple colours. Ink stained her fingers, and glitter covered her shoulders. Pottery wasn't her only hobby.

The participants were as varied as the instructors' bodily decorations. Moms and daughters seated at the tables working together. Older children and teenagers on their own. And a few men concentrating furiously on their hands.

The class wrapped up twenty minutes later and Blair waited until most of the students left before approaching the instructor.

"Excuse me?" Blair stepped to the left, so she came into view of the instructor tidying up her material.

The instructor first smiled, then frowned. "You're not in the class."

"No, I'm not. I sat in the back. I hope that's okay."

"I assume Georgia at the front desk let you in."

"She did. I'm Blair Marshall." Blair stuck out her hand.

"Clara." Slender fingers shook Blair's. "What can I do for you?" Her welcoming smile returned.

"I wanted to ask a couple of questions."

"Oh?" Clara finished putting things in her canvas bags and straightened, crossing her arms over her chest.

"Did you have any visitors to your classes in June? I doubt they would have partaken. Maybe someone watching from outside the room? Or inside?"

"June? This is about that murder, isn't it?"

"Related to, yes." No one needed to solve the murder. There was already more than enough proof that Scott and Luca killed Mason. It was the why and the reason they were in Firebrook Blair was chasing. Not the murder.

"Those guys were in the library a few times." Clara lost her rigid stance, leaning against the old thick desk at the front of the room. "They didn't come into my classes. Not after the first time. They gave me the creeps, so I told them they had to participate or get out. They left. But they kept coming back."

"For all of your classes?" Blair hoped to narrow down the list.

"Most of them."

"Which ones?"

Clara scrunched up her nose. "Sorry. I say most of them, but it wasn't specific classes. They hovered near for at least one class of every program. We were getting ready to call the cops to complain."

"Did you ever see them anywhere else in town?"

"Around the school." Clara's shoulders hunched forward. "I run classes at the school as well during the summer. I'm the art teacher there during the school year."

"Are the classes for kids?"

"They all have different levels, like the ones I do here."

"Did you recognize them from anywhere other than Firebrook?" Clara was a common denominator so far. Although Blair still hadn't checked out the rest of this street.

"I don't leave town often. When I do, there's a reason I'm focused on. Like medical appointments or shopping. I'm not paying attention to the people around me." Clara grabbed her bags, hefting one on each shoulder. "I'm sorry I can't be of more help."

"Don't be sorry. This was very helpful, even if not yet clear. Thank you so much for talking with me."

Clara's smile warmed. "You're welcome. If I think of anything else, I'll let you know. Staying at Bearbrook, right?"

"I am." Word spread about her quicker than she'd thought.

Blair followed Clara from the room and paused. The distraction of her class gave her relief from Noah. Although she didn't feel eyes on her at this moment, she couldn't shake the tingling under her skin. Noah must be near. She didn't trust this feeling.

Shaking herself off, Blair stepped out onto the sidewalk outside of the library. The municipal building sat across the street. The police station next to it. And at the end, taking up a cul-de-sac of its own was the school.

Information surrounded her. But so did people. Scott and Luca had to be looking for someone. Not something. Not an item. No one had caught them searching residences or business. They followed Clara from class to class. They were looking for Clara or someone they thought she could lead them to. Which was anyone in town based on the classes she taught.

A person who someone connected to both Firebrook and the bar Poppy used to work at.

The sun beat down on her as she walked back to the main street to *Poppy Mack's*. Tiredness slowed her limbs. Tingles erupted under her skin when *Rockhard Bears* came into view. She blinked away the image of Noah in the woods. She wanted him. But was he near? Or was this her own body reaching for what she wanted?

After a deep breath, Blair realized her caffeine buzz wore off, and Poppy made an excellent Irish coffee.

That was the reason she'd use to bombard her friend and drill her with questions for the umpteenth time.

N oah made it through the morning climbs. Even with a smile on his face. Tavis had taken it upon himself to punch him one more time between customers, stating Noah looked like he needed it. That was the last time he asked his brother to help redirect his thoughts.

He needed lunch and a beer. *Poppy Mack's* was the only place to get both. Although the food was the newest addition to their partnership. It was a welcomed addition by the town. Until Poppy showed up, many feared they'd be left without a bar at all.

Poppy made not only the bar lively, but Mack too. Noah hadn't seen the old man smile so much in years.

A blast of air conditioning hit him in the face as he opened the door, and it was followed by the scent of his mate.

She sat at the bar with a mug and half a sandwich in front of her. Seconds was all it took for her spine to straighten and for her to turn around.

Tavis walked around Noah and made his way to the bar. Noah had stopped short. He hadn't realized how deep the panic in him had run until he saw her sitting there, safe and whole.

Slow steps carried him around the tables. His brother had sat on the end and occupied Poppy in a conversation while Noah took the seat next to his mate. Fuck space.

"Hi, kitten."

Her breath shook. "Noah."

He opened his mouth to ask where she'd been this morning, but remembered it wasn't his business. Would she allow it to be his business when they mated? Whether she wanted to or not, it would be. Every move she made would be his business. He'd rather she find a safer way to do her job. But Noah knew he could never ask her to. As long as he convinced her to include him. What was so wrong with watching her back?

Nothing, if you asked him. But everything to her, it seemed.

They stared at each other, leaving the argument from this morning playing back in the air between them.

"I told you not to follow me." She tore her gaze away, wrapping her hands around her mug.

"I'm here for lunch. Just like you."

"I'm here for Irish coffee." She took a sip. "Lunch was Poppy's idea."

"Poppy had a good idea." Anything to keep her in one place long enough for him to be near her.

Mack set down a bottle in front of Noah. He didn't need to ask what he drank. Since bringing in all new stock, Noah had set himself on the mission of trying everything twice. He was still running through the list and Mack was the one keeping track.

"Thanks, Mack. Can I get a club too, please?"

Mack nodded and gave the order to one of the servers to take back to their kitchen. Their new kitchen with all new staff that Mack hated.

"I didn't follow you in here, Blair."

"And what about this morning?"

Noah frowned. "I'm sorry. I'm worried." That had been the only reason he'd stayed in the woods. He'd left with every intention of going home, but when he thought about what she was doing here, he couldn't. He'd been on his way out when she'd raced back up the gravel lane and slammed her car door.

Blair sighed. "You still shouldn't have followed me."

Noah opened his mouth to deny it, but Poppy interrupted them. "Okay, I can give you five minutes, but Blair, I've already told you everything I know."

"Poppy, they were looking for someone. A person. Not an item, or land, or any of the other theories the police had. Was there anyone that worked at the bar with you that might have even mentioned Fire-brook? Have you come across anyone in town that you recognize?"

Poppy narrowed her eyes and focused on the bar top. For all her certainty that she'd already told Blair everything, she gave the question serious thought.

"No. I haven't recognized anyone in town and I don't remember anyone ever mentioning it. Blair, you were with me most of the time I worked there. Do you remember anyone?"

Blair shook her head. "Maybe they worked there before you."

"Maybe. Or maybe they never worked there at all." Poppy reached over and squeezed her friend's hand. "How did you discover they were looking for someone?"

"At the library. They staked out classes there and at the school."

"You were at the library today?" Noah wanted to know where she'd been, worried she was off on her own in the woods somewhere, searching for leftover clues from the murder scene. Completely helpless and alone.

Blair turned her head and frowned at him. Her twisted lips held disbelief. But she didn't answer him.

"I have to assume they didn't find who they were looking for since they stuck around after the murder." Blair ran her thumb up and down the handle of her mug.

"So the person never showed up to any of those classes. It's a dead end." Poppy shrugged, then smiled at a customer who sat at the other end of the bar. She squeezed Blair's hand again, then left.

"It's not a dead end." Blair mumbled into her coffee before taking a sip.

"Blair." Noah let her set the mug down, then used his finger to turn her chin toward him. "I didn't follow you this morning after you left the woods. I went to work."

"But I felt you."

He ran his thumb over her bottom lip. "I wanted to follow you, kitten. For more than one reason."

"Will you really give me space?" She tilted her head, and he ran his fingers up her cheek.

"I'll do my best. But at the first sign of danger, I'll be stuck to you like glue." If she wasn't chasing clues, he'd have a better chance of giving her the distance she wanted. It wouldn't be easy, but easier than it was now.

"Like glue? Really?" A smile played on her lips. Noah leaned forward as if to catch it.

"Can you think of a better analogy?"

"Definitely." Their lips brushed, the light touch like static shock. It was enough for Blair to pull away for a breath.

Mack cleared his throat, waiting while holding a plate. A blush spread over Blair's cheeks as she smiled at Mack. Noah wanted to pull her back, wanted to say never mind to the sandwich Mack held out for him. But even this would fall under the category of *space*.

"Thanks Mack." He took the plate and set it in front of him. Blair faced forward again and picked up her sandwich.

He let the silence pass, neither taking long to eat. Once Poppy took their plates, Noah gripped Blair's knees and turned her on the stool to face him.

"Come over for dinner again tonight?" He kept one hand on the outside of her thigh and leaned his elbow on the bar.

"I don't know."

"I can give you some space and time, but staying apart won't help you solve your issues." He spoke low. Tavis and Poppy could likely hear bits and pieces of their conversation, but they were both considerate enough to stay out of it, unless otherwise asked.

"*My* issues?" Wide eyes stared at him under high brows. Word choice wasn't his strong suit, but it was the truth.

"Yeah, kitten. I don't have a problem with what Fate gave me. This is Fate's gift, but she doesn't control how I feel. Or what I want." Noah gripped under the edge of her stool and pulled until her knees met the edge of his. "And I really want to hear you purr again."

O h, she could purr right now if they weren't in public.

Blair knew he was right. She'd been apart from him for weeks now, and it didn't make a difference in how she felt. His confirming her suspicions changed nothing either. She still wasn't convinced that Fate wasn't playing them like a flute, but she'd never find out if she didn't give a relationship a chance.

"Okay. Dinner." The only promise she was willing to make was dinner, despite her core clenching for all the things he could do to her.

Noah pulled her in for a kiss, a full kiss. Not a light touch that had shocked her all the way to her toes. His teeth nipped at her lip as he pulled away. "I wish I could suggest skipping the afternoon and start that dinner now, but I can't. I need Tavis to punch me again so I can get back to work for the afternoon."

"You need him to do what?"

Noah grinned and winked as he stood. Tavis passed them, rubbing his hands together. "Best damn day of my life. No retaliation."

"I never said there was no retaliation. Just none today."

Tavis shrugged. "I'll take it."

The two brothers left, but not without one last look from Noah at the door. A look that said he wouldn't let her get away with just dinner.

"You okay?" Poppy appeared on the other side of the bar. The lunch rush was in full swing, but she seemed to have a lull in orders.

"Yeah. I think so."

"It's hard to trust something you can only feel."

"I should be able to trust something I feel. But I don't know if those feelings are my own or fabricated."

Poppy grinned sideways. "Enjoy dinner tonight." She left to check on the customers still sitting at the bar.

Noah wasn't the only one that needed to get back to work. Blair wanted to solve this mystery and put it behind her. That had always been her goal, not that she didn't enjoy the chase. There was a thrill that fitting puzzle pieces together always gave her. But this one was almost personal. Personal adjacent.

She waved at Poppy and left to sweet talk the police officers across the street from the library.

Blair reached for the door, but it opened. And the man she wanted to see held it open for her.

"Hello, Officer Coates." Henry Coates had been instrumental in June when dealing with Scott and Luca. Although the shifters had an advantage when searching for dead bodies and chasing down cars with women locked in the trunk. They'd worked closely with Officer Coates.

"Miss Marshall. I'd heard you were back in town. Another vacation?" His eyes narrowed, but his lips twitched.

"It is a beautiful vacation spot." Blair stood in the doorway, blocking him from going in and forcing him to continue to hold the door open.

"It sure is."

"I was actually on my way to see you."

"Were you, now? Well, I'm about to take my lunch, so it will have to wait until later."

"Or I could join you." Blair brightened her smile and stepped back inside. "Another of Poppy's Irish coffees wouldn't be a bad thing."

Officer Coates inclined his head, politeness winning. He knew she wasn't here on vacation and Blair didn't have the energy to pretend otherwise.

He stood beside an empty booth and gestured for her to sit first. She really could acquire a taste for these kinds of manners.

A server hurried over, and Officer Coates ordered his lunch and her coffee.

"Thank you."

"You're welcome. Now, what is it you wanted to speak with me about?"

"I noticed all the security cameras outside of the library, the municipal building, and the police station."

"Yes," he drawled.

"I'd like to look at the footage from June."

Henry blinked, stunned into silence for several seconds. "No."

Blair only smiled. She hadn't expected him to say yes the first time she asked. In fact, she didn't expect to look at them at all. All she needed was for Henry to look at them and then tell her everything he saw.

"Why do you want to look at security footage?"

"If I tell you that, you're going to tell me to stop what I'm doing."

"I can tell you that, anyway."

"True. But you want to know what I know. And I want to know what you have access to."

Henry lifted his arm to call over the waitress. "Can you put her coffee in a to-go cup, please?" He glared at her and Blair smiled back.

"Have you ever had her Irish coffee?"

"I'm on duty."

"That's not what I asked."

"Yes. I have. It's a favourite."

"I knew you were smart." Blair took the cup from the waitress and set some cash on the table. She couldn't let the kind officer pay for her drink now when she intended to use one to bribe him later. "Enjoy your lunch."

Blair left.

So, she wouldn't see the footage today. It was a process, and she could force the patience for it. She might be able to get it another way if Henry dug in his heels, but she liked to save that resource for other things.

Sitting on a bench in the centre park, Blair pulled out her phone.

"If it isn't my favourite reporter. Your latest episode was entertaining as usual, but not live."

"How would you know, Sam?"

"You speak differently when speaking to the people you know are listening or only speaking to a microphone. You lack a spark."

Blair hadn't realized. It was never her intention to be anything other than genuine.

"Don't worry, Blair. I have an ear like no other."

She sighed with relief. He wasn't wrong about that.

"What do you need from me this time?"

"Employment records for *Brew Stop*. Dating back to, well, I don't know when." She'd only had Sam look into the owner before, thinking whatever had been in the safe only pertained to him.

"You got it. It will take me a little while, though. I assume you want details on the employees, not just their names and when they worked there?"

"Please."

"I'll see what I can do. And this goes without saying, but our usual deal still applies."

"You'll get your cake, Sam." Blair shook her head with a smile. Their deal was a simple one. She bought him a cake any time he did a job for her. Any cake, but it had to be from one particular bakery on the south end of the city.

"Then you can count on me, gorgeous. No more than a week."

The waiting sucked, but if it gave her answers, she wouldn't argue. Sam always worked as fast as he could. "Bye, Sam."

Blair hung up and enjoyed her coffee while people watching everyone crossing the park. And not imagining what would happen when she walked into Noah's house.

Chapter Eight

One more strike to the jaw from Tavis and knowing he'd get to see Blair later helped Noah get through the afternoon. He enjoyed the young family of three. It took some time, but the young teenager warmed up to him and declared they'd be back before they left Firebrook. That kind of excitement and joy was what they'd based their business on. They wanted to share the adrenaline with anyone who was willing.

This time for dinner, Noah bought steaks and barbequed. He had everything cooking when he heard Blair's car pull up. Shutting the lid on the barbeque, he rushed to meet her at the front. He opened the door as she raised her fist to knock.

"Hi, kitten."

"Oh, that smells good."

"This is a meal my cousin does better, but I have talent." Noah wrapped his hand around her wrist and gently pulled her inside. He shut the door and lifted her hand to his lips. The kiss to her palm raised the temperature in the room by several degrees.

Blair's eyes widened and her breath caught. She looked up at him with so much confusion and desire. He could help with both if she'd trust him. Trust him when he said this was all him and his choice. But that didn't help when she didn't trust her own choices.

He didn't doubt for a moment that if Blair hadn't wanted to come tonight, there wouldn't have been anything Fate could have done about it.

"You look great." She was wearing a simple summer dress, but it flowed in all the right places, only giving glimpses of her figure. The figure he wanted to trace again as soon as possible.

"Thank you." She licked her lips.

"There's wine in the kitchen." He let her go. If he didn't, they'd never make it to dinner and the steaks would burn. Noah didn't give a damn about the food anymore. But that wasn't the purpose. The purpose was building the trust and relationship between them. And for Blair to learn to trust herself.

She followed behind him as he walked to the back deck, but veered toward the small kitchen. He'd already opened the bottle and set out a glass for her.

Noah brushed more sauce on the steaks and flipped them for the last time. The potatoes he'd wrapped in foil sat on the top rack, staying warm.

"What would you have done if I hadn't wanted wine?" Blair sunk onto one of the patio chairs, her glass half full and perched in her fingers.

"You can have whatever you want. The wine will keep."

"I know you're not always this agreeable." She spoke with warmth, her smile soft.

"I'm rarely agreeable, or so I'm told. But drink choices don't bother me." Noah uncovered the salad he had waiting and set it on the small table in front of her. Blair started to get up to help. "No. I have everything already out here."

"You're either prepared or trying to shorten the meal."

Noah tilted his chin down and pinned her with a look. "Both."

"I haven't agreed to anything past dinner." She was right, she hadn't. But Noah had little doubt that they'd make it to his bed sooner rather than later.

He took the steaks off the grill, setting one on each plate along with the potatoes. He set them on the table but didn't take his seat. Leaning forward, Noah lifted her chin with his knuckle. "Are you telling me you're going to dine and dash? Because that I won't be so agreeable to."

"I didn't say that." Her whispered breath touched his lips.

"Blair." He growled her name and changed his grip, sliding his hand around the side of her neck.

Blair straightened her spine, putting her lips in contact with his. Noah kept them as they were, her sitting and him leaning over her. If he let her stand, they'd take this too far. Her hands had a white-knuckled grip on the arm of the chair.

He let his tongue explore hers, and she opened up to him with a sigh. The growl from his bear grew intense. It would be difficult not to mate her tonight, but he'd have to stop himself. Doing so would destroy the bit of trust she had that brought her back here tonight.

Lifting away, he clenched his jaw. "Time to eat." The words came out as more of a harsh command, but Blair didn't seem bothered.

She nodded and settled back into the chair.

Noah let the tension fade before he spoke. Anything out of him would be incoherent. His bear stalked beneath his skin. The first bite of the steak surprised him because it wasn't his own teeth tearing at the meat, but the sharper ones of his bear. The ones he'd use to sink into her skin when they mated.

"Can I still come for a climbing lesson tomorrow morning?"

"Absolutely." He'd wondered if she'd still want to. But if he'd learned anything about his mate, it was that she never gave up.

"Am I taking someone else's slot? You asked me only a few days ago. You must have been booked up."

"Don't worry about it. No one else will miss out. Tavis can handle it."

"If you're sure?"

He pointed his fork in her direction. "Don't be late." There wouldn't be a chance for her to be late. They weren't spending tonight apart.

She grinned and finished her salad.

"What did you do this afternoon?"

"Had coffee with Officer Coates and then made a phone call."

"You had coffee with Henry? Just catching up?"

"Something like that."

Noah forced himself to stay quiet, but hoped with everything he had that she'd open up to him.

"I need access to the outside security footage from the library, the municipal office, and the police station."

"He didn't agree, did he?"

"Of course not. But that isn't the point. I need him curious enough to look himself. If he lets me look too, then that's a bonus. I don't need to see it, I just need to know what's on it."

"Clever kitten." He hated to admit it, but she was good at what she did. And Henry will fall right into her trap. He still puzzled over the entire incident from time to time.

"I know." She grinned up at him, pride shining in her eyes. She loved her job.

Since meeting her, he'd listened to her podcast religiously. She reported everything with heart, but never something that she couldn't prove. What he hadn't yet done was listen to the older episodes of *Blairable*. After hearing about her not so hypothetical situation of being locked in a basement, he wanted to know how much of her experience she reported in cases like those.

"What was your phone call?"

She glared for a moment before answering. "Confidential."

"I see."

Fuck. He wanted her to stop. But only because of the danger she put herself in. It was a purely selfish desire. He didn't want to lose her before he even had her.

He'd be one hell of an ass if he asked her to quit. She was good at this and proud. As she should be. This was a career she'd built on her own, built her reputation, and gave no one reason to doubt her.

Noah had to let this go. If he pushed, she'd shut him out.

They finished eating and Noah couldn't take his eyes off her. A pink tinge filled her cheeks from the food and wine. Her eyes glazed with the spark he'd lit when she walked in the door. It had never fully distinguished.

"Don't dine and dash." He hadn't meant to beg, but he sounded desperate.

"I'm not." Her decision was in her voice. Noah only hoped she realized it was *her* decision.

He stood and held out his hand. As soon as she put her hand in his, he clasped his fingers around it and never planned to let go.

Blair must have imagined the tremor in his hand before he wrapped his fingers firmly around hers because he looked down at her with fierce eyes. Noah didn't let his gaze roam over her body. No, he focused on her face with an intensity that took her breath away. It was unsettling.

He pulled her up and into the house, not stopping until they reached the bedroom. She may have let on that her only intention had been dinner, but she wasn't stupid. She knew they'd end up here. More than an hour had passed with her sitting in the park, circling herself around her own thoughts and feelings. Trying to decipher what came from her heart and what Fate had implanted was nearly impossible. It all came back to her wanting him. Simple. Black and white.

"Close your eyes, kitten." Noah spun her, so she stood at the end of the bed, facing him.

"And miss the show? No, thanks." The last time she'd closed her eyes for him, the heat running through her had been overwhelming.

"Just for a bit. Close your eyes." He stood a foot from her, her hand still in his, and waited.

With a shaky breath, she did as he said. Blair focused on every inhale so as not to focus on his touch or the pounding of her heart. Being forced to acknowledge the thrum of whatever this was threatened to weaken her knees.

Noah let go of her hand and clasped both of her wrists. Pulling them up, he put her hands together above her head. But that was the last conscious movement she followed.

Warmth traced down her arms and sides. Cool air brushed over her skin, starting at her legs. Noah lifted her dress oh so slowly, so that every inch of exposed skin first cooled, then inflamed.

"Blair." He said her name like a prayer before pulling her dress up her arms and dropping it to the floor. His lips brushed her neck, sending tingles down her spine to a particularly odd place on the left of her lower back where nerves sparked to make her core clench.

Even though he'd taken her dress off and didn't hold her arms up, she couldn't move them. Noah cupped her face and kissed her, sliding his hands to her shoulders and pushed her arms down for her.

He slipped his arms around her, his hand skating up her spine. With a grip on her hip, Noah pulled her hard against him. His clothes felt rough over her sensitive skin while he thrust his hips against her. A slow rolling rhythm.

Blair's breath shook as he set his lips to her neck. Up and down, he nipped and kissed until her knees were weak. She had to grip his shirt to help hold herself up. Her fingers went numb from the tight grip.

Backing her up to the bed, Noah eased her down. Her eyes flew open. She pulled his shirt with her until she lost her grip.

Feeling that he still wore his clothes and seeing them made something click. He was still dressed, and it didn't look like his next goal was his own clothes.

His fingers grazed her legs as he slid her panties down her legs.

Noah looked down at her with such reverence that doubt forced its way into her heart. She didn't doubt Noah, but doubted how Fate could control this. Genuine emotion was etched in his features, in the glow of his eyes.

Fate wouldn't allow time for reverence. Blair was sure She'd want a mating frenzy, uncontrollable ripping of clothes and fast, pleasurable fucking. Blair had felt that frenzied state before. But this wasn't it.

Noah pulled her to the end of the bed and lifted her feet. He knelt on the floor and set her heels on his shoulders.

"Give me everything you feel, kitten." He set his tongue against her clit and worked her with the same methodical reverence he'd started this with.

Blair had to be fair. She had to give over to the night, give herself over to Noah, and allow him to show her the truth. His truth, not Fate's. And maybe she'd find hers.

Pushing her head back into the mattress, she closed her eyes and fisted the bedding.

His fingers played in her folds, circling her entrance before moving away. He drove her up slowly, teasingly. But his tongue was focused and consistent.

The frenzy threatened her, but didn't seem to touch him. Blair dug her fingers in his hair, trying to force him to give her more. He fought her, not letting her control even a second of this.

"Not until you come." The heat of his breath only teased her more.

"I need more to come."

"No, you don't."

Oh, fuck. He was going to tease her into an orgasm. Her thighs shook, but she could feel the edge. Not yet. But she knew it was going to be sharp. How could it not be when he forced her to focus on every single sensation he gave her?

Noah moved one hand up her outer thigh to her hip. She hadn't realized she'd thrust against him until she felt the bruising grip of his fingers.

"Please, Noah."

"Beg for it again, kitten." His growl vibrated through her.

She whimpered and arched her back as her entire core quivered. She didn't need to beg again. His demand, his harsh voice against her centre, ignited the climax that had been clawing its way out of her body.

Noah chuckled. "That's what I wanted to hear. Good kitten." He licked at her entrance before standing up.

Blair panted and watched him strip as slowly as he'd stripped her. "Hurry," she whined. An honest to God whine. But Noah looked pleased. His sexy mouth lifting to one side.

"Do you feel the difference yet, Blair?" Noah undid his jeans and pulled himself out. He left his jeans on his hips while he waited for her answer.

Blair had a hard chest and a long cock to distract her from focusing on the truth of what was between them.

"Blair?" He set his hands on his hips and cocked his head.

She licked her lips and moved her gaze back up his body. "Fate isn't in this room right now. That's all I can say for sure."

"She isn't even under this roof. This is all us. All me. All you, kitten."

Blaire nodded.

"Good." Noah shoved his pants off. "Move up the bed." He followed her as she scooted until her head rested on the pillows.

"Noah." She took three full breaths. "I want..."

He held himself above her. "What is it you want?"

Blair licked her lips and looked down. His responding growl was worth it.

Blair's lips glistened from her tongue and her eyes dilated as she looked down between them. His cock ached. Never had he been this hard and ready for someone in his life.

She finally understood. Or she at least saw what was here when Fate wasn't. And that fractured his methodical control on the night.

But now she looked at him with hunger, and Noah wanted to give her the world.

"Say the words, kitten."

"Please."

"I don't need manners. Say it."

Her hands slid down his chest, turning halfway so she could wrap her fingers around his cock.

"You're anything but shy, Blair. Give me the words, and I'll give you whatever you want."

"I want to suck your cock, Noah." She pushed on his chest and he obeyed her movements. It was the only control he could give her tonight. He had the urge to move up her body and keep her head propped by the pillows.

It was only fair to let her explore without Fate's interference.

Noah landed on his back and tucked his hands behind his head.

Blair took her time running her hand up and down his shaft. Mischief sparked in her grin.

"Don't you dare try to tease me. It won't end well."

"A threat? I'm not sure I can see a downside to teasing you."

"You want to stay where you are? Don't tease."

"And where would I end up if I keep teasing?" She hadn't stopped her slow strokes as they talked, even using her thumbnail to lightly scrape over the head. The sensations were strong enough to make him grind his teeth.

"I can think of a lot of different positions for this. And none of them give you free use of your hands."

Blair paused.

"No teasing, kitten."

She nipped her bottom lip, but lowered herself to take him into her mouth.

Noah tensed. Her wet heat eased over him until he hit the back of her throat. She still didn't tease him. With an easy rhythm, Blair moved up and down, squeezing the base of him with one hand. But despite his warning, she still swirled her tongue around the sensitive spots on the head.

The last thing he wanted to do was lose control and give her any doubt. If he didn't have his hands clasped behind his head, he'd have them in her hair.

Just the thought was enough to make his hips jerk. He hit the back of her throat on his own and cursed, settling back against the bed.

"Blair." He let out a plea as desperate as hers.

She sucked harder, and he lost it.

"Tell me stop if you don't want me to do this." Noah gathered her hair and fisted it in one hand. He used his other hand to hold the side of her head.

Her mouth pulled at him and she swirled her tongue. She didn't bother trying to escape his hold to give him any other answer.

Lifting his hips, he fucked her mouth with shallow thrusts. But only enough to bring him to the edge and stop. He pulled her off him.

"Get on top of me, kitten." Only for a few minutes. He was too close to give her full control. Because he wasn't done with her yet.

Blair moved and Noah held himself ready for her.

She closed her eyes as she lowered herself. Her chest expanded and froze with her held breath.

She was a fucking goddess.

Noah met her every thrust, cherishing the way her body quaked.

His eyes heated. The change was harsh and sudden. The details of Blair and the room around her came through with immense clarity.

"Noah," she gasped.

"It's okay, kitten."

She didn't stop, but she didn't look away from him.

He tasted blood and realized his teeth had sharped, cutting his inner lip. With the magic pumping through him, he healed almost instantly, but the implication of those teeth tightened his grip on her hips.

With a growl, he flipped them over and took over with a punishing force.

The same mating instincts must have filled Blair because she tilted her head to expose her neck.

"Do you know what you're offering, Blair?"

Shock widened her eyes, and she straightened her head. Noah locked his elbows to keep himself away from her. No matter how much he wanted to run his teeth down her neck to tease her with the idea of belonging to him.

"Be sure before you offer it again. The next time, I'm claiming."

She tensed.

"*I'm* claiming. Me. Fate doesn't make my decisions for me. When I sink my teeth into your neck, it will be because we both want it."

Noah rolled his hips and set up a brutal pace. But not once did their eyes leave each other. The sensations sliding down his spine intensified from her gaze alone. All of it burrowed itself in his core, waiting to explode. Waiting for the right moment to let go.

"Noah. It's too much." Blair shook beneath him and then shut her eyes, cutting off the power between them.

"No." He gripped her chin and stopped thrusting. "Open your eyes."

"I don't want to."

"Yes you do, kitten. Open them."

Slowly, they fluttered open, and he moved again. She whimpered, her back arching to take him deeper.

"Everything, Blair. I'm here for everything. For always."

A tear slipped from the corner of her eye. Noah wiped it away, choking down the thickness of his own emotions.

The climax took them both by surprise, exploding with a terrifying ferocity that shattered his soul.

Fate be damned. She was it for him. Blair was his mate, his match.

Chapter Nine

The robust aroma of caffeine woke her. Hot, strong, and the only thing guaranteed to pull Blair from the bed. After the blissful hum and pleasurable aches, she was having a hard time remembering what she should be doing.

"Good morning, kitten." Noah's deep voice sent fresh shivers through her body. Fresh, delicious, warm shivers that gave her more reason to stay in bed. But the caffeine sank deeper as she pulled in a breath through her nose.

Cracking her eyes, she looked toward the bedroom door. Noah stood there in only a pair of boxer briefs and holding a mug. His physical nature was unfair to the rest of the world. But to her? She was one lucky woman.

Blair blinked the thought away. They hadn't mated. She wasn't lucky yet.

"This is for you." He stalked across the room and Blair was lost again in the sight of his body. He sat on the side of the bed and held out the mug.

Tucking the sheet under her arms, she sat up. Noah scoffed at the sheet, but let her take the coffee, anyway.

"Half an hour. And then we're leaving."

"Leaving?"

"Your climbing lesson, remember?" His lips tipped up. Then he left her to drink alone while he disappeared into the bathroom.

Her climbing lesson. The last one had barely registered. Oh, she remembered every minute, but she hadn't retained any information regarding climbing. She retained a solid image of Noah, every muscle, his scent, and the sound of his voice. Blair would never forget the day she met her mate.

Her head had been filled with fanciful thoughts of a sexy man until she'd learned what they were and had learned about mates.

The coffee was slow to sink into her system and she still felt as if she was waking up when Noah came out of the bathroom. Last night had eased the stress their relationship caused. And part of her wasn't ready to let that go.

Maybe she didn't have to.

His towel sat low on his hips. Why the hell did guys do that? Did it have to be that low? He smirked when she let her eyes drop down and back up. They must do it on purpose, knowing the effect they have.

Setting her almost empty cup on the nightstand, Blair let the sheet drop and crawled toward him. The towel hit the floor, but Noah stepped back.

"No. We're going climbing." He backed up to the closet, eying her like she'd attack from the bed.

"Fine." Blair hopped off the bed and locked herself in the bathroom. Because she wanted to attack him and keep their time hidden away in here going.

She rushed. If she didn't, her thoughts would sink back into reality, leaving the night behind. The night where he showed her something other than Fate. He showed her himself. He showed her what her own heart was screaming at her.

Hair braided and body dried, Blair walked out of the bathroom with nothing on, moving straight to her clothes from the night before. Noah sat on the end of the bed.

"I don't think a dress will work for climbing."

"We'll run up to the cabin so you can change." His eyes did the same as hers when he came out of the bathroom, roamed her body and stopped at the apex of her thighs.

"No time." She slid her dress over her head.

Noah chuckled and stood. He had his arm around her before she moved out of his reach. Damn, he moved fast. He kissed her, soft and swaying at first, but then he devoured her, bringing back to life everything from the night before.

Her heart beat a different rhythm. It beat with a warning, a truth, a prayer. She didn't want to let this man go. Blair wanted to wake up every morning with him, climb every rock with him, wanted to talk to him every night until they fell asleep. Wanted to love him. She did. Not Fate. Not an aura she couldn't see. Blair Marshall was falling in love.

Lifting his head, he set his forehead against hers. They panted together, and he locked his eyes on hers, as if he could read her every thought.

Without a word, he steered her toward the door.

* * *

Her thoughts had come through loud and clear. Not word for word, but Noah felt the moment the truth sank into her, the moment she realized she loved him too. Fuck, he couldn't hold back much longer. If either of them had said another word, he would have toppled her back to the bed and mated her. And he couldn't be sure that she would have stopped him.

As much as he wanted to stay in that bubble, he wanted to spend time with her outside. He wanted to show her more, to show her everything they could be together.

They'd driven up to her cabin in his truck and he waited while she ran inside to change. It was safer that he'd stayed in the truck.

Now at *Rockhard*, he had her around the back, sizing the harness for her. Tavis cleared his throat from the back of the main building.

"Good morning."

Blair turned and smiled bright. That smile sucked people in. And Tavis was no different. He strolled over immediately.

"It's nice to see you again, Blair." Tavis knew damn well he'd be seeing a lot more of her. His brother inhaled, long and quiet, but Noah didn't miss it. The two of them scented strongly of each other. The aroma wasn't only sex and lust. Noah had scented the beginning strands of mates after their kiss in the bedroom. They'd bonded.

There was no going back now. Only forward.

"You, too. Are you joining us?"

"Afraid not. I have a couple coming in soon."

"I'm sorry. I hope Noah isn't leaving you stranded?"

"Of course he is."

Noah growled at his brother.

"But I don't mind. Don't worry yourself, Blair."

She glared like she intended to go against him.

"Which trail are you using?" Tavis started pulling out equipment for his lesson.

"The North trail." The trail they rarely used because it was a longer hike and with a busy schedule, they didn't have the extra time to hike between lessons. It gave Noah the privacy he wanted with Blair.

"We'll see you two for lunch, then. Have fun." Tavis hefted the rope over his shoulders and hung the harnesses and loops with the carabiners on his arm. He winked at Blair before sauntering to the front of the building.

"Ready?" He'd put each of their equipment in backpacks and passed one to Blair.

Slinging it on her back, she nodded. "Ready."

They could get where they were going with one of the side-by-sides, but the bear inside him wanted the air. Tourists rarely used the North trail, but there was a turnoff that most didn't know about. A safe spot where they could shift after a climb.

"How long of a hike is it?"

"About two kilometres." Short by most standards for a hike, but being off the beaten path, it wasn't easy.

Blair's body was lean under her curves. He'd seen what she was capable of when she was here in June. The hike and climb would be no trouble for her.

As the trail became more rocky and thick, they moved to walk single file. Noah stayed behind Blair, ready to help her where needed, but of course his mate didn't need any. The muscles in her legs worked to lift her up and carry her over every obstacle. Her balance was perfect.

They didn't talk—Blair concentrating on the trail and Noah concentrating on Blair. He could hike this trail in his sleep.

Half an hour later, the trail opened up to a sheltered clearing. A rock face expanded around a hill while trees hovered over them to create a serene cavern. The rock was perfect for beginners, so this wasn't a place he and Tavis used to climb often, but the space itself was comfortable for their bears. Just outside of town, but unused and easy places to hide if someone happened upon them.

Blair stopped and looked around, her hands on her hips. "Is this it?"

"Yes."

"There's an echo." She laughed and smiled wider as the sound spread and came back to her.

"Take a break. Get some water."

She nodded and took the backpack off. Leaning against a tree, she pulled out the water and sipped slowly.

Noah didn't rush her. He drank his own water and waited until she came to him.

"You'll need to refresh my memory. That day is a little foggy."

"Foggy?"

"I only remember you from that day."

Noah ran his finger down her jaw. "Me too." They were lost in their first meeting, the moment Fate made her wishes known. "Let's get the harness on you."

He'd shown her back at the building and she quickly fastened it in all the right places while Noah put his own on. Once finished, he took the time to check it over.

"Good. Now, let's get up there." He pointed to the rock. It was short compared to most, but Blair's eyes still widened.

"Let's do it." Her heart beat faster and she licked her lips. Maybe nerves, but she was full of excitement.

He went over all the equipment and what they used each piece for as he put it all in place. He attached her chalk bag, anchors, and carabiners, to her waist.

Staying at the bottom of the cliff, holding onto his end of the rope, he directed her up. This time, he had more focus on teaching her and not forcing himself to focus on safety so he didn't get distracted and hurt his newly discovered mate.

"You're doing great, kitten."

"This is so much fun. I knew I'd had fun last time. But this is better."

"Much better. Ready to go higher?"

"Yes." Enthusiasm made her answer echo. She took a moment to look around from up there before catching his gaze.

"You're gorgeous."

"I know." Her eyes sparkled, and she lifted one shoulder as much as she could while holding on.

Noah nodded back to the rock, then guided her to make it to the top.

"I did it!" She gave a bounce.

"Yeah, kitten. You did. I'm coming up now." Noah focused on getting himself up while Blair took a seat on the grass.

It took him half the time to reach the top. And when he did, he pushed Blair down on her back and held himself over top of her.

"Caught you." He kissed her, licked at her lips until she opened. He pressed her into the ground, breathing in the mixed scent of his mate, the earth, and his home.

She broke the kiss, but only to whisper against him. "I didn't know it was a chase."

He laughed. "A chase is fun."

"Is that an offer?"

"You wouldn't get far, kitten."

"A head start might make it fair."

The adrenaline through Noah's body spiked. Hard and fast, his blood pumped and his bear roared. Never did he intend to have a chase like this with Blair. Hadn't thought he'd crave such a game, but the moment the idea came from her, an excitement he'd never known existed thrummed.

"A ten-minute head start?"

"You don't know what you're getting yourself into, Blair." The use of her name made her pause. He saw it in her eyes and heard her heart skip a beat. She was reconsidering, but it didn't last long.

Wriggling, she made her way out from under him. He didn't have the willpower to stop her.

She took all of her gear off, dropping it next to her backpack while holding his gaze.

"Kitten." His voice had changed. The deeper growl of the predator escaped.

Her breath shook, but she continued to drop her gear until she stood straight and waited.

"I'm counting."

She smiled and ran. The small cliff was only one side of a grassy hill. Blair raced down and turned further North.

Noah breathed deep, not wanting to let go of her scent in his nose. His ears pricked, the instincts of his bear taking over. His mate was on the run and he needed to catch her. Part of him worried what would happen when he did. His control might slip. It was slipping now. The game called to his bear, who was more than happy to play, except it wouldn't be a game for long.

Time was passing and Noah had no idea how much. He waited as long as he could and then pushed himself further.

When he finally did move, he tore his equipment from his body, discarding it next to Blair's.

He intended to yell out, *ready or not*, but a low, rumbling roar escaped instead.

He was going to catch his mate.

Oh, what the fuck had she just done? She poked the bear and now had to deal with the consequences, but those consequences excited her. No thinking. Blair forced every logical thought from her mind and only focused on the ground in front of her.

Her body had already been covered in a fine layer of sweat that the breeze had dried and refreshed her while she'd waited for Noah, but the moment he'd laid her out, her temperature spiked. She wanted him. She wanted more of him. The real him. The other half of him that controlled how he felt about her. She'd gotten the man and his truth the night before. Now she wanted the truth of his animal.

Her feet hit the ground hard, and she forced her feet to be lighter. *Think light thoughts, Blair.* The point was to get caught, but not too soon. She didn't have it in her to make this easy.

The air vibrated with his roar and she gasped. Her time was up, not that she'd been keeping track of it. She only moved further away from town. Further away from the trail. Noah wouldn't be a man when he caught up to her.

His eyes had already changed before she got out from underneath him. Glowing round orbs in narrowed spaces. An enticing mix of colour that they'd almost made her stop. Just to admire them.

Twigs snapped, and Blair paused. She couldn't hear anything else over her breathing, making her think she must have imagined it. Would Noah allow her to hear him? Bears were big, but she'd bet money that shifters knew how to stay silent.

She started running again. The trees were thick enough to hide another rock face until she almost ran into it. Blair squeaked and threw her hands out to brace her landing. She bent her elbows until her chest touched the rock. This one was longer than the one they'd climbed. She had nowhere to go except back the way she came or to follow the rock.

But a huff from behind her froze her in place. Now she heard his steps stalking closer. His nose touched the middle of her back, sniffing quickly rather than drawing in full breaths. She frowned, but shook off the oddity.

Blair had asked for this. She was the one who started it. She needed to be brave enough to finish it.

Blair turned, and his nose kept contact, circling her body. Blair swallowed her scream. This bear was black. This wasn't Noah.

Oh shit. What was she supposed to do? She'd already given him a chance to get too close. Any time she'd gone on a hike in the past, she carried bear spray and bear bangers. Always prepared and vigilant. But she'd left all of her equipment and her backpack behind. And there hadn't been any spray or bangers in the pack because she was already on a hike with a fucking bear.

The bear moved his snout around her stomach. Her most vulnerable part. She couldn't make any sudden movements. And curling in on herself to seem submissive and protect her soft centre wasn't possible with the cliff at her back and the bear pushing his nose harder against her. She swore drool dripped from his lips.

Closing her eyes, she tried not to whimper when she felt a tooth as he moved his nose to her side.

Noah. Where are you? The voice inside her cried. She felt the tears like they trailed heat down her dry cheeks.

I'm here, kitten. Her eyes flew open, and she gasped as Noah's voice sounded in her mind. But the harsh breath startled the black bear. He tensed and opened his mouth with a growl.

A louder one ripped the air from her right. The black bear whipped his head around and turned himself to press his side against her, as if to protect his catch.

Noah was twice the size, and he instantly charged through and around the thick trees. There was nowhere for her to go to get out of the way. Digging her heels into the ground, Blair braced herself to get caught in the fight.

The black bear's weight pushed off her. Noah ducked his head and hit the bear with his shoulder. Sharp claws scraped across the side of her calf and the two furry bodies moved away from her. She held in her cry and darted back toward where Noah had been. Staying as far away from the fight as she could.

When she looked back, Noah had the black bear pinned beneath his massive paw. He bared his teeth and his eyes looked like they were on fire. He roared in the face of the other animal. Even Blair felt the warning and the threat. Every being within five kilometres could likely feel the warning.

Noah did nothing more, but she saw how much he had to restrain himself. He pushed off and stalked back and forth, waiting for the other bear to get up.

Blair kept her back to a tree, holding herself up with her hands gripping it behind her.

The black bear moved slowly, but he made his way to his feet and lumbered away with a limp. Noah kept his eyes on the bear, heaving and catching his breath. Blair didn't dare do anything. She couldn't judge the state of her mate.

Her mate. She knew it in her heart. They were more connected than she ever could have imagined possible. She'd heard him, felt his words. Felt his soul.

But he was on the edge. A terrifying wildness ruled him.

Long minutes later, he turned toward her. Narrowed eyes scanned her body, and he came closer. Noah lowered to the ground and put his face next to the wound on her leg. Blair took her first look at it. It wasn't deep, not even bleeding anymore. But it stung.

"Noah?"

She couldn't hear him anymore.

He licked the scratch. Warmth tingled over her leg. It didn't heal, but it felt better.

Noah pulled his large body up, his head level with her chest. Then he lifted his front paws, climbing them up the tree trunk on either side of her to cage her in. Towering over her was a magnificent beast.

Warm air swirled around them, seeming to move through Noah. He changed in front of her. The sounds of popping bones were so close they made her cringe. When he finished, he still towered over her, but now as a man rather than a bear. Except his eyes. Those took longer to change back.

"Are you okay?"

She nodded.

"I need to hear you say it, Blair. The words." His voice was hoarse, still so close to an animal.

"I'm okay."

"I'm sorry. I should have stayed closer."

"It's not your fault. And I'm fine. You got here in time."

"But I might not have." He lowered his head to bury his face in her neck. "Blair." He inhaled.

The adrenaline of the chase replaced the adrenaline of the scare with the black bear. Caged in by him, it came back in full force.

His cock hardened between them and he pressed himself against her. Dropping one arm, he set a hand at her hip.

"I'm not so sure I like that running game anymore." He ran his lips up and down her neck.

Blair let out a small laugh. She tilted her head, allowing him the access he'd warned her about last night. Running her hands up and down his chest, she flexed her fingers. "I think you do. I did."

A sharp tooth broke through his lips, nipping as he kissed the base of her throat. "I need you, kitten."

She knew the risk of taking this further with him, but it wasn't enough for her to stop it. She needed him, too.

"Noah, please."

Shoving off the tree, he tore her shirt over her head and shoved at her pants while she kicked off her hiking boots. It was a scramble between them. He slammed his foot between her feet and lifted her out of her clothes with an arm around her waist.

When he set her back down, he spun her around. Gripping her wrists, he pulled them up and set her palms against the rough bark.

He wrapped a fist around both braids and pulled her head back to look down at her. His eyes were his own now, but they were sharp and bright.

"I love you, Blair. I won't hide that anymore. You're mine."
Angling her hips, he thrust up, filling her while never breaking eye
contact. "I dare you to deny you feel the same way."

"Don't dare me. I never say no to a dare."

He laughed, a little of the tension fading with it. "I'm going to
remember that, kitten."

Chapter Ten

H is damn teeth wouldn't retreat. Keeping a hold in her hair allowed him to keep her away from him. The last thing Noah wanted to do was mate her against her will. He'd given her everything to prepare her.

The scare of the black bear didn't douse the arousal of their chase. At least not now that the threat was over. Their desire had gone dormant, but it had been that desire and adrenaline that attracted the young, curious black bear to begin with.

She was slick and hot around him. His grip on her hip was bruising. He had to. Letting her go wasn't an option for a long time.

Blair had closed her eyes and her lips parted in a silent scream as he took her. As much of a claiming as he dared. Her small fingers dug into the tree trunk.

"I want to hear the truth from you, kitten." Noah worded this carefully. No dares. No chance for her to turn it around. She understood the truth he referred to. He'd spent hours showing her.

"It's too soon." But she said it more like a question to herself.

"There's no timeline with this. It is what it is, and nothing can change it." Noah loosened his hold on her hair and ran his hand down her spine. His thrusts continued, measured and hard.

"Noah." She cried out and arched her back, pushing her ass toward him. He fought the urge to go faster.

"Tell me, Blair. Let go. Stop trying to hide it away."

She whimpered and dropped her forehead against the tree.

A single hard thrust settled himself all the way inside her, and he held himself there. "Blair."

"I love you, too." Tears escaped in her gasping voice.

"I know, kitten." Noah moved again, resuming his measured pace, but only until Blair looked over her shoulder at him. Rounded eyes begged for something.

Breathing heavily, she tilted her head to the left, further than he'd been holding her with his grip on her hair. She didn't break eye contact. She knew what she was doing. His teeth were still sharp and ready.

He'd lost his voice. Straining, he tried to give her one last warning of what he was about to do, but the only sound that escaped him was a growl.

Her walls quivered around him and his orgasm rushed him. The sensation had been unexpected. Moving his hand back up her spine, he held the back of her neck in the exact position she offered.

"Come." He mouthed the word, as his voice was still unpredictable. She cried out and bucked her hips in the small amount of space she had.

Noah took his own advice and let go. Leaning forward, he let his teeth graze her neck, up and down, over her shoulder. Her climax kept going and once he bit her, it would start all over again. He waited for his release. Holding it back wouldn't work much longer.

"Noah." She whimpered as her body weakened. And that sound was enough to put him over the edge.

He exploded, filling her, holding her. Opening his mouth wide, he slowly sank his teeth into her skin, prolonging the bite.

Her entire body spasmed as she reached a new high. Noah held the bite as long as the peak wracked their bodies. Arm around her waist, he held his mate tight against him.

Minutes. Long minutes later, his teeth retracted, pulling from her skin on their own. Blair whimpered, but she was weak in his arms.

Noah used the last bit of his strength to find a somewhat soft patch on the ground and laid them down with her on his chest.

He felt whole. Never known there had been something missing from him. And maybe there hadn't been until he met Blair. Warmth filled him, satisfying warmth that came from Blair. An invisible string connected the two of them. Connected them as mates. The difference was vibrant.

Stroking up and down her back, Noah waited until she roused on her own. Blair set her chin on his chest and looked up at him. Bracing an arm behind his head, he propped it up so he could see her.

"Now what?" Her eyes were hooded and her lips were soft. No regret lingered in her features, something Noah was grateful for. The moment had been intense and as soon as she submitted, there had been no stopping it.

Noah heaved a controlled sigh while tucking her hair away from her face. "Now, I go to work, and you go do whatever it is you're doing." He still hated that she chased murderers, but there wasn't anything to stop her short of locking her up and that was something he'd never do. "Then we'll pack up what you have at the cabin and move you to my place."

"Why would we do that?"

"Because you're moving in with me."

Blair laughed. Her eyes widened to hysterical proportions, and she laughed. Pushing off his chest, she stood and grabbed for her clothes.

"What are you doing?"

"Well, you need to go to work and so do I. You know, for the job I have, that isn't here."

"What do you..."

"Not in Firebrook, Noah. I have my own career and life. Mating was inevitable—I see that, and I know it wasn't Fate—but it's not that simple. It's not a sparkle of a magic wand and I walk into the rest of your expectations with a smile on my face."

"I didn't expect you to." He grabbed her shirt before she could pull it over her head. They each had a tight grip on the fabric, and he used it to bring them closer together.

"No. I'm not doing this now. Let's go." She shut her eyes and shut him out.

After letting go of her shirt, Blair shoved her arms in and pulled it over her head. She sat on the ground next to the tree and put her boots back on, never once looking up at him.

He wanted to get inside her head. Their situation was black and white in his eyes. They were mated and that meant she moved in with him. But he didn't believe for a second that would be straightforward. Difficult didn't mean it wouldn't happen. He couldn't leave Firebrook. His business, his family, his home, and the safety it provided for his kind. He wanted to raise his family here and give them the same safety. Leaving Firebrook was unimaginable. Meaning he understood all too well what he was asking of Blair.

"Blair."

"Don't." Her clenched teeth muffled her growl.

It felt as if his lungs collapsed and his throat constricted. Time. They just needed time.

While she finished with her boots, Noah shifted. He wouldn't be tempted to talk, to push the conversation, if he couldn't speak at all.

The hike back should have been quiet, but her own anger raged in her ears. A consistent, loud hum that burned.

Noah wasn't wrong, but neither was she. And that wasn't how you should go about asking someone to move in with you. But Noah did. Thinking that being fated mates changed things and made them inevitable.

A few times during the trek, Noah nudged her hip with his snout, pointing her in a different direction. She hadn't stuck to any path or recognizable features when she'd run from him. If she'd been out here alone or he hadn't walked back with her, she'd be lost by now.

Her now mate lumbered alongside her, almost as tense as he'd been when fighting off the black bear. Blair didn't let her gaze linger on him.

When they reached the trail, she picked up her pace, leaving Noah behind. He couldn't ramble on the trail in fur. But it only took a few minutes before she heard her name and his footsteps.

"Blair!"

She shook her head and kept walking.

His footsteps stopped. She refused to acknowledge the pang of disappointment, but she had nothing to say. The hum in her ears blocked out all logical thought or words. Now wasn't the time to have a discussion or make decisions.

Giving up her career wasn't an option. And he'd already made it clear he didn't approve of it. What kind of life living together would they have without support? Their best chance at staying happy would be apart. Wouldn't it?

She wanted to scream.

Her walk through town blurred. Blair thought she'd heard her name being called a few times, but nothing registered enough for her to respond. It was rude not to answer, but she couldn't have guaranteed any kindness. And most people in Firebrook didn't deserve her bad mood.

This wasn't just a bad mood, though. This was a pivotal point in her life. She was mated, and now felt a physical connection between them. Her blood hummed a little differently. The mark on her neck pulsed as she remembered every moment against the tree. Noah's teeth had pierced her slowly, stretching time, stretching the mating, the change that happened with heat and magic.

The memory worked hard to calm her, but it wasn't enough. A deep breath helped a little. Enough that she raised her head to see where she was rather than blindly continuing around town. She'd intended to go back to the cabin for a shower, but she passed Bella's Bakery heading toward the library.

The motivation to hunt down clues just wasn't in her today. Rolling her neck, she sighed, ready to turn at the next crosswalk, putting her on the right side of the road to get back to *Bearbrook Cabins*.

Two men came around the opposite corner, but promptly turned and disappeared. They'd stopped suddenly enough to draw her attention. Both wore ball caps and thin jackets. The weather hadn't cooled enough for jackets. And the ball caps were both navy blue with a white stripe on the bill. She'd seen those hats before. And the set of those shoulders, almost scrawny.

Even stewing over her mating and its consequences, Blair's curiosity roared. It couldn't be them. Those hats were a dime a dozen anywhere but here.

The light changed, showing the white stick figure. She trotted across the road, hoping to get a glimpse of them around the corner.

Damn. They weren't there.

It happened so fast and she was coming out of her head, still full of Noah. If they'd been there, she should have seen them again. They hadn't had that long to get out of sight.

Rubbing her eyes, Blair turned down toward the main street running through the centre of town. It was the quickest way back to the cabin.

Although, for the rest of the walk, she kept her head up, smiling as people greeted her. Poppy and Wyatt stood on the porch of the main lodge, coffees in hand, and Wyatt wrapped around his mate's back.

Poppy didn't go into the bar until about now and Wyatt always took an early lunch to spend time with her before she went to work. They made their lives work well together.

They waved as she passed and Blair returned their smiles, never slowing her pace. The last thing she wanted to do was talk about this with her friend before having an actual discussion with Noah. Despite the fact she could offer some guidance from her own experience. But Blair had been with Poppy through her decision to leave Firebrook and then to come back to him. She'd lived through it with her friend and had known what to expect when mating Noah. She just hadn't expected his outright assumption.

Rushing past didn't work though, not with the nose of a shifter and that of a shifter's mate. They smelled the mating on the wind. Both of their chins lifted and their expressions changed. Neither excitement nor concern, only blank, wide-eyed stares. Poppy pushed Wyatt off her and rushed down the stairs. Wyatt ambled behind her. Blair had no choice but to stop.

She held up her hands. "I don't want to talk about it yet."

"Okay." Poppy paused a few feet from her. "But is this a good thing, or a bad thing?"

"I don't know yet. But it was my choice." Blair wouldn't have anyone thinking Noah had taken advantage. She knew what she offered by giving him access. "I'm having a shower and going to bed."

"You know where to find me." Poppy pursed her lips. It hurt her not to help. And it hurt Blair to do that to one of her best friends. But her body and mind still buzzed from the experience. She needed to think before trying to navigate her next steps.

"Thank you." She aimed a reassuring smile at Poppy and then Wyatt, who looked rather solemn if not pleased.

Walk away, Blair. She didn't need that moment to stretch into awkward pity.

Once inside her cabin, she leaned her back against the door. Her hand lifted to the bite on her neck. Staring at the bathroom door put fear in her chest. She didn't know why she feared seeing the physical mark. She'd seen Poppy's. It was beautiful. But it held so much power.

Her neck heated and tingled as her fingers traced over the slightly raised flesh. It was done and even now, she didn't regret it. Blair was falling for him. That's a lie. She'd already fallen for him. But why did their future together have to look a certain way?

Gathering her courage, because she had it in spades with years of practice stomping on fear, Blair pushed off the door and went to the bathroom. She kept her hand over the mark until she was in front of the small mirror above the sink.

Her skin was flushed and her hair a mess. Good grief, what had people thought as she'd rampaged through town?

The moment of truth where she not only felt it, but saw it. Tilting her head, she slowly moved her hand away from her skin.

It stole her breath. A raised crescent marred the point where her shoulder met her neck. It was darker than Poppy's, but this was fresh. Blair had seen Poppy's after she first mated, and several times after Wyatt had bitten her, remarked her.

Blair's was pink and defined against her skin.

Mated.

Using only one finger, Blair traced the shape. Watching herself in the mirror was different. The sensation was stronger. Flashbacks of Noah's face over her shoulder swam in her vision. Like a dream cradled with the shadow of the mark. Noah's body against hers. Him filling her. Every thrust, every spasm, every ounce of heat engulfing her body. Gripping the sink with her other hand, Blair relived it while staring at herself in the mirror. She relived it all until the point of climax and the pain of the bite.

Panting, she closed her eyes. Shaking hands pulled her clothes off and started the water. Reliving the joy and contentment wouldn't help her solve their current problem.

Choosing her life over her mate.

She never came back. Noah worked for the rest of the afternoon, only taking adult male clients, people he knew wouldn't be offended by a gruff attitude. He wasn't capable of playing nice with families or children.

Tavis had taken one whiff of him and rearranged their schedule without a word. He intercepted the family that walked in the moment Noah got back. The family he'd been supposed to take out.

Noah didn't remember helping Tavis close. His gaze hadn't left the front door or the street. He scanned the trails leading to *Rockhard*. Blair never came back.

He gave her time. In the end, she'd come to the same conclusion. They couldn't be apart and why not live together? Why waste time searching for a solution when the best was right in front of them?

She feared losing her career. Noah understood, but she didn't have to lose it. It may not look the same anymore, but despite his dislike for the danger she put herself in for her job, he'd never ask her to quit. He would have told her that if she'd stuck around long enough to talk.

At home, he did everything to keep himself from going after her. He showered, cleaned his house, even did administration work for the business. They didn't have a secretary and didn't want one. Sometimes, they'd ask their cousin, Dakota, to help during busy seasons, but for the rest of the year, he and his brother took turns.

It wasn't his month, but he sat at his kitchen table with his laptop, going through schedules and expenses, anyway. Because it kept him from leaving his house.

She should be at the cabin. Safe inside. And alone. Noah had no reason to think otherwise.

But she wasn't with him, and that was the problem.

Midnight rolled over on the clock and he groaned. Storming from his house, he walked to *Bearbrook*. The night air smelled fresh and was enough to douse the adrenaline pumping through his blood. And walking through town gave him a sense of calm, knowing that everything was as it should be and nothing out of place.

Except his mate.

Reaching her cabin, he paused and inhaled. She was inside and alone. His fear disappeared. But his need for her only grew. Listening, he heard her footsteps.

Before he knocked, Blair opened the door.

"Hi, kitten."

"Don't *kitten* me." She shut her eyes and turned away from the door, leaving it open for him to come in. It was all the invitation he needed. "I'm not re..."

Noah cut her off. "No. I don't want to talk right now." He grabbed her wrist and swung her around so she landed against his chest.

Her hair hung around her shoulders, wavy and out of place, as if she'd allowed the air to dry it after a shower. He watched his hand as he ran his fingers through her hair, letting the strands slip through the cracks before starting again, but the second time, he brushed it over her shoulder. Her breath caught as he bared his mark.

"I want to look at it." With his thumb under her jaw, he tilted her head further. A perfect crescent, slightly raised and light pink. It would continue to fade and blend into her skin tone until he marked her again. It wouldn't disappear. They were mated.

"Noah, how could..."

"Shh." He cut her off again. They needed to talk, but it could wait. If all he'd done hadn't yet convinced her, then he'd show her more.

Leaning down, he ran his nose along her neck and inhaled her new scent. A delicious mix of her and shifter. The sweet scent of a mate.

His tongue lashed out of its own accord, licking the crescent. Blair froze in his arms and goosebumps pebbled her skin.

"I don't want to feel this right now."

"And what is it you feel, kitten?"

"So good." Her hands fisted in his shirt. "But please, I just want to figure this out."

He couldn't deny the pleading in her voice. "Okay, but I'm not stopping."

Blair whimpered. Noah let his hands drift to her ass and he lifted her. Moving to the couch, he sat down with her straddling his lap. His hand on the back of her neck, he pulled her down, his mouth continuing the assault on her neck.

"Talk, Blair."

"You just assumed I'd move in with you." Her hips moved against him. Noah clamped his other hand on one to stop her.

"What's the alternative?" He grazed his teeth down her neck and over her mark. She shivered.

"Not living together." Blair bowed her back.

He chuckled. "And how do you think that will work?"

"This doesn't count. It's still new, vibrant, and oh so hot. Time will help."

"Have you asked Poppy if time has dulled their bond? What about Bonnie? I know of several other shifters and their mates you could ask too." Noah placed open-mouthed kisses on her as he spoke, using his tongue with each one until her spine melted.

"You don't know what you're asking me to give up."

That stopped him. "Don't I? You think I haven't considered what it would be like to give up everything here?"

She blinked down at him. "Yes, I think you have. But..."

"There's no but, Blair. It's the same. I understand. But it won't change anything to fight it and search for a solution. It will only waste time. Time that I want to spend with you. Just. Like. This." He pulled her down to crash them into a kiss. Noah drank in her air, pulling her gasp back out of her and into his own lungs.

Her hips moved again, fighting against his hold. He let go. If her own desire and emotions were going to take over and take them further, then he shouldn't stop her.

Relaxing against the couch, Noah gave over to her. She hadn't even realized he no longer controlled the kiss. Not yet.

Her hands pulled at his shirt and delved underneath. She undulated on him, running her centre over his cock. The urge to free himself was too strong. Noah set his arms on the back of the couch and gripped.

She slowed, lifting her head. Blinking, she looked at his arms. "Is something wrong?"

"Nothing's wrong. Take me, kitten. Do what you want. But I ask one thing."

"What?"

"Let go. More than you did the other night. Don't let your worries affect this. Let go, kitten."

"You won't... you're not..." The poor thing was confused. Noah grinned.

"I'm not moving, for now. I won't be able to hold back for long. So you better make the best of the time you have."

Chapter Eleven

B lair eased her hips against him once she registered what he said. It didn't make the assumption right, but he wanted her to feel. Wanted her to acknowledge this bond between them.

Because that mattered. Those emotions impacted their decisions.

Could she stay away? Could he stay away if she did? Or would they crash together in the middle on their way to reach each other?

Blair didn't have the answers. Lifting her shirt over her head, she did as he asked and let go. It was her core, her instincts that told her what to do. Her heart beat with a guiding rhythm.

Noah tensed beneath her and his eyes heated. Undulating her hips, she moved up and down his erection. She could overthink this. Take her time and tease him in the same ways he teased her. She could fulfill fantasies she didn't know she had. But his knuckles turned white from the grip he had on the back of the couch. There wasn't enough time for fun.

Pulling at his shirt, she lifted it up. Noah took over, grabbing the back of the collar.

There was too much distance. Too much to think about. Blair needed a solid connection. Standing, she stripped off her pants, rushing to kick them off her feet. As soon as she climbed back onto his lap, she kissed him. Cupping his face and the back of his neck, she devoured him. It was heady, being the one in control of a kiss. Deciding when to shift, to lick, to sup.

Blair pulled his bottom lip between her teeth, and Noah growled.

"Careful, kitten."

She laughed, light and free. The worries of their mating gone for the moment. His erection jumped, reminding her of her end goal. She'd been having fun simply kissing him and dragging out the pleasure.

Reaching between them, she undid the fly of his jeans, shoving until she had his cock free. Running the tip through her folds was all it took for her to crack. Blair lined him up and slid down.

"Fuck, Blair. You feel so good."

She whimpered. Setting her forehead against his, she moved. The grip on his shoulders gave her the leverage she needed, but it wasn't enough. She couldn't get them any further, any higher.

Moving faster, she became frantic, trying to chase something she couldn't find. She heard fabric tearing and snapped her eyes to Noah. He was rigid against the couch, but he didn't give any indication of what had made the sound. Looking at his hands, she saw the back cushions held claw marks, the white stuffing puffing out of the tears.

"Don't stop, kitten." His voice was rough, carrying a familiar vibration.

"I can't do it. It's not enough." She started moving again, but still something was missing. It was his control, his touch that she needed and decided in that moment that she could never live without.

He tore his hands off the back of the couch and gripped her hips. He lifted her farther than she could and rolled her hips in a way she hadn't thought she had room to do. Meeting her thrust for thrust, he filled her. Pleasure met pain, and she dug her nails into his shoulders, sure she'd leave marks.

But wouldn't that be fair? For her to mark him the way he marked her?

The pleasure grew, jumping off the plateau she'd created. Even so, the climax was out of reach.

"Let go, Blair. You're still thinking too much."

Was she? It was difficult not to. But it wasn't their living arrangements crossing her mind.

Noah reached his thumb toward her centre and pulled up the hood covering her clit, exposing it so each thrust ground against her.

"I don't know how to let go."

"You do. You've done it before. This is us, Blair. All the pieces will fall together as long as we're together. It's that simple. Simple doesn't mean easy. But I won't live without you. Can you say you can live without me?"

Blair whimpered, not wanting to answer him. Not wanting to make commitments she couldn't keep.

"Damn it, Blair." He wrapped an arm around her waist and flipped them, laying her out on the couch. "Come, kitten. Give me everything you are."

He had one hand cradled behind her head and his fingers tightened. His eyes pierced hers. The heat overtook her and the mark on her neck flared with a delicious pain.

She broke. Like lightning snapping in her ears. Her body convulsed, clamping tight around him.

"Noah." She cried out, but her voice sounded like a faraway echo.

"That's it. I've got you." He froze inside her, holding still as his climax took hold.

The last thing she remembered was his lips gently touching hers as her eyes fluttered closed. Noah wanted her to let go, but Blair didn't want to let go of this.

S un shining and birds chirping. That's how Blair woke up. On the couch with a thick quilt tucked under her chin. Who knew orgasms could wear a girl out? She didn't. This was a new development Blair could get used to. A cure for insomnia—as long as her mate was around.

But her mate wasn't around now. A harsh energy surrounded her when he was near, especially now that they'd mated.

Blair peeled the blanket off and pushed herself up. She stretched her arms straight up, the cool morning prickling her skin. And that's when she remembered she was still naked.

How had he done that? Noah had commanded her body in a way she couldn't understand.

The coffee table had been empty last night, but now there sat a single folded piece of paper. With a key on top. Blair lifted the key with a sigh.

Maybe he was right? Or were they both right? Simple was an over exaggeration of their situation. But if you take away all the muck in the middle, isn't the solution still simple? Move in with him. She travelled a lot for work, anyway. Home was always a temporary thing for her.

Opening the paper, she read it.

My home is your home, whether or not you're in it. I love you, kitten.
- Noah

Simple.

Well, if she wanted simple and time to focus on a new life, whatever that may look like, she had a job to finish first.

Blair grabbed her purse from the counter and pulled out her keys. She added the key to Noah's house, then went straight to the shower. A decision would be clearer when she didn't have this mystery looming over her.

Work brought her here, and now she needed to focus.

Easier said than done, but she dressed, and cloaked in her imaginary armour, Blair hopped in her little car and headed to Bella's Bakery. Caffeine first—always.

The line was long, the last person holding open the door while exiting customers squeezed by. Blair debated her need, but she wasn't in a hurry and every single thing out of that bakery was worth the wait.

When it was her turn to hold the door at the end of the line, the weight disappeared from her back. Spinning her head around, she saw Henry Coates, his arm above her head, with his hand wrapped around the metal edge of the door.

"Good morning, Miss Marshall."

"Good morning, Officer Coates." She'd hoped for a chance meeting with him rather than having to track him down and turn into a nuisance. Although she made a damn good nuisance when needed.

The line moved a little slower than normal, but Blair wouldn't begrudge anyone the delectable treats made with care behind that counter. Bonnie, her mother, and their crew could take as long as they needed. But as they inched forward, she felt the heat of his stare on her back. Looking over her shoulder, Henry's gaze met hers.

Blair tried not to smile as she faced forward again. Every few minutes, she'd look over her shoulder. He stared down at her with narrow eyes. As if his thoughts turned into whispers. She'd learned to sense the anticipation of a conversation. And as those narrow eyes got thinner, Blair let her face burst into a grin.

He sighed. "What made you think those two would be on the security footage for those buildings?" He spoke low so that the others in the coffee shop wouldn't hear enough to catch the entire conversation. But it was no secret why Blair came back to Firebrook.

"You looked." Blair faced him, her arms crossed over her chest.

He didn't answer her, but the twitch around his mouth said enough.

"Hey, Blair. What can I get you this morning?" Bonnie called from the other side of the counter. Blair turned around, her smile still in place. She'd finally get somewhere with her search today.

Henry stepped up beside her. "Hers is on me this morning. And I'll take my usual, please."

Blair turned to him. "Thank you, but you don't need to do that."

"It's policy to supply the coffee during an interrogation." Mischief filled his face, chasing away some of the suspicion.

"Well then, maybe I should buy your coffee."

He chuckled and shook his head, handing Bonnie his card before Blair. With the line still growing behind her, she figured this wasn't a battle she needed to win. She gave Bonnie her order and thanked Henry again with a nod.

Outside on the open sidewalk, Blair took a deep breath. She didn't envy Bonnie and anyone else having to work inside a hot bakery during the summer. Air conditioning or not, it was too stuffy.

Henry hadn't moved far from her, sipping his coffee while frowning.

Blair cocked her hip and smirked. "I'll tell you mine if you tell me yours."

For the second time, he didn't hold back his chuckle. "Follow me to the station, Miss Marshall."

"Blair. Please."

He nodded once and walked away toward his patrol car. Blair pictured herself doing a victory jig inside her head. As much as she'd love to clack her heels together, Henry watched her until she got into her car.

However, she allowed herself to wiggle with excitement in her seat for the three-minute drive to the police station.

Carrying their coffees, they met at the door. Henry held it open for her. "My office is at the back."

"I remember."

Henry shut them in and took his seat behind his desk. The chairs in front of it were well worn, but the leather was still smooth. Blair sank onto the edge and leaned forward toward his desk.

"Where did you see them?"

He tilted his head and stayed silent for a moment. Damn, he wanted to control the conversation. Blair held back her disappointed sigh. She'd get all the information one way or another, but this would be a lot easier if he'd involve her from the start.

Blair sat back in the chair, letting her eagerness fall away.

"Why don't you start, Miss Marshall."

"Blair," she corrected quickly.

"Blair. What made you believe those two would be on the security footage for the buildings on this street?"

The library, the municipal office, the police station, and the school. "Because they'd been spotted at both the library and the school often."

Henry frowned. He hadn't known that.

"My turn. Were they on the footage for all four buildings?"

He didn't want to answer if the pinch to his lips meant anything. But he nodded anyway.

"How often?"

"No. My turn again."

Blair smirked. She could work this way.

"Who saw them at the library and the school?"

"Clara. They staked out a bunch of her classes at the library. And a few at the school."

"Classes? What classes?"

Blair raised her brow, a reminder of the rules of their game. "How often do they show up on the footage?"

"Daily at the school and the library. Every other evening at the municipal offices."

"As if they were looking for a way in." Blair didn't phrase it as a question so that they could still carry on. He nodded.

"What classes?"

"All of hers."

Henry's calm snapped. "What the hell were they looking for?" He didn't direct the question at her.

Blair set her coffee on his desk and leaned forward. "No more question for question. Show me the footage and maybe we can figure this out together."

He hesitated, but conceded and stood. "All right, Blair. But you need to tell me everything you know."

"Deal."

* * *

N oah hadn't heard from her all day. He'd wanted to give her space, the time to think. But as evening approached, he grew impatient. His bear grew impatient.

He left work and went straight to her cabin. He didn't have to knock to know she wasn't there. The silence settled over the small building. When there was no life inside, a place lacked an essence—a scent and sounds.

Noah drove around town, with no sign. Closing his eyes, he tried to feel her, unsure if their bond extended that far. Far enough to feel distress.

He knew where her next steps were. And she'd been hoping to hook Henry Coates's interest. Logically, that's where she'd be. He drove to the police station. A few of the officers walked out the door, leaving for the day, but Blair's car was parked behind Henry's.

Noah nodded to the officers as he passed and headed straight inside to Henry's office to find it empty. Voices echoed from the back of the building. He followed the sound and saw Blair and Henry hunched over a computer.

"Here." Blair pointed at the screen. "He's holding something in his hand."

"I hadn't seen that, but right about now, he's going to try the door handle." Hook, line, and sinker. Blair had snared Henry into the mystery. That helped Noah feel better about her chase. Henry wouldn't let anything happen to her. As long as she included him in the rest of her search. That was the kicker. Blair was too independent to rely on someone else.

"He's not just trying the handle. He has both hands in front of him."

"He's trying to pick the lock without making it look like he's picking the lock." Henry squinted as he leaned even closer.

"What time of day is this?" Blair asked.

"Just after closing."

"Are they on any of the other cameras about twenty minutes before this?"

Henry looked at Blair a little wide-eyed, realizing what she was getting at. Noah cleared his throat to interrupt them. They both jumped.

"Noah. My apologies. I didn't hear you come in."

"That's all right, Henry. You two are busy, I see." He met Blair's eyes over Henry's head. It took a few seconds for the thrill of their chase to fade away. Once it did, her eyes softened with unspoken words. All the things left unsaid by him leaving in the middle of the night last night. All the things that him leaving her a key to his house did say.

"Yes, Blair is convincing."

Blair? Henry took a while to be on a first name basis with new residents. And he didn't yet know that Blair was a new resident. Or would be. In some form. He hoped.

"I can't take all the credit. Henry is as curious as I am."

Henry? Noah had missed a lot in a day. His bear grumbled under his skin, not liking the closeness of the two of them. He knew there was nothing to worry about. Not before they'd mated, and not since. It didn't matter to his bear, who wanted their mate alone and to themselves.

Blair tapped Henry's shoulder. "The footage."

"Right." Henry clicked on the mouse. Noah moved in behind them.

"Across the street at the library. But they're facing the municipal offices."

"Until Georgia leaves. Then five minutes later, they're trying the door as if it might still be open." Henry sighed. "That's clever timing."

"What do they want in the municipal offices?" Noah frowned at the screen, refreshing his memory on the build and size of the two men. Not that he'd forgotten a single detail about the two who'd threatened his mate.

"They're looking for a person. I'm sure of it," Blair stated with a fist on the desk. Her emphatic certainty was contagious. She had instincts that most couldn't understand. She'd roped Henry and pulled him onto her trail.

And Noah. Even he wanted these two caught and dealt with. He feared it might cost him his mate. He feared any story she chased would cost him his mate. But he couldn't deny what she was good at. It wasn't just her curiosity. Her intuition and ambition were limitless.

"I think you're right. A person they'd expect to find at the library or the school. The municipality has resident records." Henry tapped his fingers on the desk, staring at the paused footage.

"We should start with employees at the school." Blair turned toward Henry. "Teachers, support staff, janitorial staff. And cross that list with the classes at the library. I can ask Clara if they keep records of attendees."

"No need." Henry let the old chair fall backward until Noah was sure it would hit the floor. "Just ask her if anyone from the school takes her classes. She'll remember."

"They staked out the classes she taught at the school, too." Blair twisted her lips. "That might open up a whole other pool of people."

"True, but this is a place to start."

Blair nodded. "I'll talk to her tomorrow."

"No." Henry sat up and pinned Blair with a look. "I'll talk to her tomorrow. I'm afraid you're done with this search, Miss Marshall."

"Oh, we're back to Miss Marshall now?" She scoffed.

"I'll share information with you when I can for your story. But I won't allow civilians to put themselves in danger. Again." He gave her a pointed look. Blair had been in the thick of the danger in June. Noah didn't need the reminder.

Blair only smiled and patted Henry's shoulder as she stood. "I guess we'll see who gets to the library first. Have a good night. *Henry.*" She let her hand drift over Noah's stomach as she left the room.

Noah was stuck to the floor. She was magnificent. Confident and brilliant. And that meant Noah would always be there to watch her back. His future had already changed, but everything shifted for a second time as he realized how determined his mate was.

"Have a good night, Henry." He clapped the other man on the back and followed his mate.

"Try to talk some sense into her."

"I have other battles with her I need to deal with first."

"I just hope those two don't come sniffing around again."

That made two of them.

Chapter Twelve

B lair gently lifted herself from Noah's bed the next morning. He'd caught her with a hand on the back of her neck in the parking lot of the police station. Spinning her around, he'd planted his lips on hers.

"I missed you today," he'd murmured against her.

Blair had missed him too, the feeling always there in her core, but she'd been thoroughly distracted searching for clues with Henry. By the time they'd finished eating dinner, Blair had passed out on the couch. The screen fatigue had caught up to her.

She had no memory of going to bed, but realized that Noah must have put her there. Now, as dawn had crept over the horizon for the past hour, she tried to leave without him waking.

"You're not quite as stealthy as a kitten." His gruff voice mumbled against the pillow. Blair disagreed with that statement, but it was only because of what he was.

"You have an unfair advantage." She stopped beside the bed.

"Mmm." He leaned up on an elbow and rested his head against his hand. "You're trying to beat Henry to the library, aren't you?"

"Of course."

"Promise me something." Noah stretched across the bed, gripping her wrist and pulling her back down. She sat on the edge of the bed while he curled his body around her. "If you have any reason to believe they're back in town, you come find me. Immediately."

Blair bit her lip. She'd thought she'd seen them the other day, but had chopped that up to her mental state. She hadn't focused on anything other than Noah and they'd disappeared so fast; she was sure she'd imagined them.

"Blair." Noah sat up and gripped her chin. "I mean it. I want to know."

Still, she said nothing. She couldn't make that promise and not tell him about what she thought she saw.

"Fuck. They're already here." He let go of her, but didn't back away. Somehow, he seemed to grow without moving.

"I don't know. I..."

"Tell me, kitten." His voice may have softened, but his body didn't.

"I thought I saw them the other night. Walking home from here. I wasn't paying much attention to anything around me. And they disappeared so fast. I'd convinced myself I'd imagined them. When I went after them..."

"You did what?" A dangerous rasp took over Noah's words. Blair clamped her lips tight. "Oh no, don't stop talking now. Why don't you finish what you were saying?"

"I don't think I need to. The point is, I only saw them for a split second. It could have been anyone. Or my imagination." It was best not to remind him of her lack of awareness and that she hadn't even realized where she was in town until that moment.

Noah ran his fingers along her jaw to the back of her head. He speared them into her hair and grasped. "New promise, kitten. Promise me you won't chase them and if you have any indication where they are, you come find me right away."

She shook her head, but Noah tightened his hold.

"There's only one answer. I won't be able to breathe until you promise me."

Blair leaned into his hold. The last thing she wanted was to cause him pain. She hated to make the promise. It wasn't one she could guarantee. But if it helped him, she'd promise him, knowing he'd be able to sense the untruth to it.

"Okay. I promise." She let her lips tilt up.

Noah glared. He didn't believe her. But that was okay. She didn't want him to believe her.

She pulled against his hold, but he moved with her. Leaning toward him, she kissed him. But she didn't get past the first touch before he rolled her back onto the bed.

No build up, no foreplay. He settled between her legs and pushed into her.

"It doesn't matter what troubles we have between us. I can't survive without you, Blair." Raw emotion ripped from his throat. Blair felt every word like a harsh strike, settling themselves into her core as if they were her own.

The tether linking them together strummed, vibrating their connection. The peak overtook them with a harsh explosion. Blair screamed, not expecting the sudden onslaught.

Noah roared and buried his teeth in her neck, creating a new mark on the other side.

It started a ripple effect, weaving out of him and into her and back again.

They laid together until calm air refilled their lungs. Noah lifted her from the bed and carried her to the shower. They didn't speak another word until they were both clean, dried, and clothed.

"Be careful, kitten."

"I will. Always."

Noah kissed her and then walked her out of the house, opening her car door for her.

His voice replayed in her head while she drove, and waited in line for coffee, and still echoed while she carried the tray with three coffees into the library.

Clara wasn't there yet, but expected any minute. And five minutes later, as Blair expected, Henry walked in behind her.

Pulling one coffee out of the tray, she offered it to him with a smile. She'd thrown down the challenge of a race. Blair would have been disappointed in him if he hadn't shown up first thing.

"Good morning, Blair." He smiled grudgingly and took the coffee.

"Good morning, Henry." She decided not to ride him about calling her Blair again rather than Miss Marshall. Best not to push her luck too far. As long as law enforcement found her charming, they tended to be helpful.

When Clara came through the door, a large tote on each shoulder, neither of them rushed to speak to her. They waited until she set her bags down behind the counter and let out a sigh.

But Blair was the first and even had an incentive. She held the coffee across the counter.

"Good morning. Is that for me?" Clara looked almost startled by the two of them standing there.

"It sure is."

"Thank you. That's so kind."

"You're welcome, but I'm afraid it comes with more questions." Blair scrunched up her face.

Clara took a sip with closed eyes. "Anything for one of these." She sighed. "You told Bonnie this was for me, didn't you?"

"I may have asked her if she knew your favourite."

"You are a clever woman. I'm all yours." She cocked her head toward Henry. "Hello, Henry. I assume since you're hovering so close, you're interested in any answers I have as well?"

"I am."

Blair hid her grin, but looked up in time to see Henry roll his eyes.

"Are any of the students in your classes from the school? Teachers, support staff, or janitorial staff? If you don't remember, do you keep records of your attendees?"

"I remember. And yes. I've had a few students that belong to the school. On and off for years. Earlier in the summer, I had a couple teachers and the school secretary."

"Lillian and which teachers?" Henry stayed a step behind while taking part in the questioning.

Blair had to admit, searching for information in a small town was simple when everyone knew everyone. But what would that search look like if you didn't know anyone? Like Scott and Luca?

"Yes, Lillian Rose, Quinn West, and Harper Bardot. You don't think they're in danger, do you?"

"No. I'm just searching for the connection." Blair squeezed Clara's arm. The truth was, she wasn't sure if they were in trouble. If Scott and Luca were back in town, they had unfinished business. What did they want with a resident of Firebrook?

* * *

* * *

"Thank you, Clara. Can we come talk to you again if we have more questions?" Henry spoke gently. Blair didn't react to his use of *we*.

"Absolutely. Anytime."

Henry walked her out, veering her straight to her car. "I'll let you know if I find any connection to those three women."

"Or I can help you look for the connection." Blair leaned her body against her car door, stopping Henry from opening it.

"Don't push it." His tone firmed, but a new fondness lurked around his lips. She was growing on him. But she wouldn't take things too far and ruin that. Besides, she had her own resources.

Henry walked across the street, straight for the police station. Blair sent off a text to Sam, asking him to run those three names against the list of employees from the bar. She didn't expect any of them to have worked there, but there should be a connection.

Sliding her phone back in her purse, she looked around. The town was just coming to life, but the streets were still mostly bare. The occasional person walking to work or driving by. Peacefulness engulfed the air. Blair tried to imagine what it would be like to live here permanently.

A dream.

Blair paused while reaching for the handle of her door. Two figures emerged from the back of the municipal offices. She ducked. Instinct ruled her motion for the moment. They didn't disappear in a flash like they had last time. There was no mistaking who they were. She hadn't imagined anything. Scott and Luca were back. Blair could chase clues all she wanted, but the only ones with answers were the two of them.

They hadn't spotted her right away, but it only took a few minutes for them to spot her car. Blair watched them through the windows, hoping they couldn't see her peeking. They spoke to each other before making their way to her car.

Shit. There was no way they wouldn't see her. She had to drive a compact car too low to the ground for her to fit underneath. They split apart the closer they got, each taking a direction around her car. All in a moment, the streets were bare. Blair was all for following them and finding answers, but she didn't have a wish to get caught by anyone. Sure, it had happened more than once and it didn't stop her from doing her job when the next story arose, but she didn't willingly jump into the fire. Okay, sometimes she did, but getting caught by them now didn't have any advantage.

She needed people. Reaching into her purse, Blair thumbed her key fob, finding the bottom button. Holding it down, she waited until her car blared obnoxiously.

Scott and Luca froze, searching around them. She watched the curse form on Scott's lips before he gestured for Luca to follow him. They jogged away, slowing as they reached the next corner.

Blair left her alarm going while she chased after them.

Her promise to Noah rang in her head, louder than her car. But she refused to lose them.

Once she reached the corner, she dug into her purse to turn off the car alarm. She heard voices behind her, people stepping outside to investigate the sound, but Blair ignored them. Peeking around the corner, she saw the two men walking, trying not to bring any attention to themselves. They turned toward the centre of town, but turned again soon, leading them to the west side. Away from most of the lodging available. They couldn't be stupid enough to stay in town. Everyone here had long memories.

She was about to follow them around the next corner leading toward the west residences when a hand gripped her arm.

Noah spun her until she landed against his chest, then cupped both of her shoulders to hold her. "What's wrong?"

Blair bit her tongue from cursing at him. "Nothing's wrong." Except she just lost Scott and Luca. "Why would you think something is wrong?"

"Your car alarm."

When she only blinked at him, he continued.

"Word travels fast. I heard the alarm, but someone came down to say it was your car."

People had noticed her connection to Noah.

"I saw Scott and Luca. I was hiding behind my car and they were coming toward me. I needed to scare them off."

Noah's eyes narrowed, and his jaw tensed. "You were following them."

Any answer she gave wasn't a good one.

Noah inhaled and then set her behind him. "Go tell Henry and stay inside the police station."

"You've got to be kidding, Noah."

"Now, Blair." He stalked away in the direction Scott and Luca had gone. She needed to talk to Henry, but at least if she finished following them, she'd have solid information to give him. Like a location of where they were staying would be great.

She stared at Noah's disappearing back and let out a frustrated growl of her own. Then she ran through town to get Henry.

N oah would deal with his mate later. The putrid scent of the two men was faint in the air, but he recognized it well. Despite differing from anyone he knew in town, their stench was branded in his memory from the moment he attacked them on the highway and pulled Blair from the trunk of old Mr. Abernathy's '57 Chevy Bel Air.

Their trail led him through the houses in the northwest of town. The incline of streets set the neighborhood above Firebrook. And that's where he lost them. They'd weaved in and around streets and at one point, Noah was positive they'd split up. Either out of caution or they'd spotted him or Blair.

Fuck. He may not find them now, but he'd be back. A search in fur with his stronger nose and in the cover of night would find them.

Noah followed the scents for a few more minutes, then went to the edge of the neighborhood and stood in the treeline. They hadn't come this way since he started following them. Yet. They'd passed here before. Noah knew where he'd start his search.

Taking the shortest route down the hill, he headed straight for the police station. Henry stood outside, talking to the other officers over the roof of his car. One of them pointed toward Noah. Henry turned around.

"Did you find them?"

"No, but they were in the northwest neighborhood when I lost them." He didn't need to clarify that he lost the scent rather than sight.

"Patrol that area for the next few hours," Henry ordered the others.

"May I make a suggestion?" Noah leaned himself against the hood of Henry's car. "Keep searches discreet. They won't slip up and allow themselves to be seen again if they see you all out in full force." Noah wanted them caught, not spooked and running.

Henry nodded. "Brady and Parker. Get in street clothes and spend some time up there. I'll monitor footage around here and even install some more cameras to catch blind spots. The rest of town can have regular patrols for now. But stay vigilant. Catching them is the priority." He looked at Noah. "Thank you. We better go let Blair out."

"Let Blair out of what?"

Noah caught the man's smirk before he turned away and stalked inside.

"Hell to pay, I say! This is unlawful. I swear *Officer Coates* better watch his back." That was Blair's voice echoing through the small building.

Henry led him down the back hallway toward the three cells the station had. Blair stood in the centre, feet shoulder width apart and her arms crossed tightly over her chest. She glared at the floor outside the cell until their feet came into view. Then she raised her head.

"Payback is a bitch, Officer. Henry. Coates."

Noah laughed. He laughed hard, bending forward at the waist. He couldn't help it. The sight was the most perfect thing he'd ever seen.

"Really, ma.... Noah?" The word mate almost falling from her lips hitched his laughter, but didn't stop it.

"I couldn't have come up with a better plan myself." Noah clapped Henry on the shoulder. The other man looked like a cross between satisfied with himself and terrified of Blair's wrath.

"She refused to stay behind."

"She didn't tell you she was already chasing them when I found her, did she?"

Henry turned his head toward her, dropping his chin. "No."

"Are you going to let me out?" Blair still hadn't moved from her centre position.

"I'm not sure I should." Henry leaned against the wall. "Not only are you chasing after them after I've said not to, but you've just threatened me."

"Officer Coates." Her voice dripped with sweetness. Noah was enjoying the show. He rather liked her safe behind bars. "You wouldn't know where to look now if it wasn't for me. Noah knew which direction because he found me. You need me. As much as I need you. So you're safe from my threats for the time being."

Noah would have tracked them without her first following, but Henry couldn't know that.

Henry shook his head and stepped up to the bars, pulling keys from his pocket. Unlocking the door, he stood in the way of her getting out. "Please don't get yourself hurt, Blair." He stepped to the side and looked over her head at Noah. "Keep her out of trouble."

"I'm trying." Noah took her hand, entwining their fingers as they walked out of the station.

"You didn't have to laugh so hard," she said through gritted teeth, a sulking sound in her tone.

"I'm sorry, kitten. I couldn't help it." Instead of taking her home, which he knew she'd hate, he took her out to lunch at his cousin's restaurant. The place was busier than ever this year and that might have something to do with the softer side of the owner that came out since finding his mate.

Most of Firebrook often compared Noah to Caiden. Both men were a little more grumpy around the edges than needed to be.

Caiden joined them at their table for a few minutes—long enough for Noah to fill him in on what had just happened. They made unspoken plans through a look. Noah would have help to search for them later. Not only from Caiden, but his brother Wyatt, too. Poppy had been their target back in June.

"Barbeque at the lodge tonight." Caiden slapped the table as he stood. Those family and neighborhood barbeques happened at least once a week. Another reason Noah couldn't leave. There was a connection to his family and his land that was indescribable. But more than that. It was something he wanted to share with Blair.

"We'll be there." Blair answered.

Noah nodded to his cousin, then turned to his mate. "Avoiding being alone with me?"

"Never." Sarcasm dripped from her lips, but she blushed while mischief danced in her eyes.

Noah paid at the bar on the way out, then turned Blair to the path through the woods that led back to Bearbrook cabins.

"I don't need to go back to the cabin."

Noah had a few reasons for her to go back to the cabin. Tucked away in safety was one. Packing was another. But he didn't need to bring up either. "I know."

"Then why are we going there?"

"Because there's nothing else to be done today." Not until tonight when he could go hunting.

"Not good enough." Blair cut across the path in front of him and veered off toward the main street. "I'll spend time at the bar with Poppy."

Noah followed, shoving his hands in his pockets. The bar would have to do. He still had climbers to look after that afternoon. And he'd worry less as long as she was tucked away inside somewhere.

They stopped at the back door. Poppy would let her in through here with only a text from Blair.

Blair set her hands on his chest, but Noah kept his tucked in his pockets.

"I'm not hiding. Or being locked up." Her eyes flared with new anger at Henry. "This is what I do. You can't protect me from this."

"Blair, you're my mate. I will protect you from everything. Losing you isn't an option. Ever."

A sad smile settled on her mouth. She tilted her head and pulled his down. A gentle kiss that tasted sweeter than her exploded on his tongue. It was over too soon. "I'll meet you at the lodge tonight."

She knocked on the door, and lucky her, it swung open. Mack frowned at both of them.

He heaved a sigh. "I'm regretting going into business with a twenty-something year old."

Chapter Thirteen

W hen Blair told Poppy about the barbeque, because apparently it hadn't been planned past Caiden's invitation to her and Noah, Mack offered to close the bar. But Poppy wouldn't let him work alone. She assigned one of the new hires to him for the night. He grumbled and glared, but Poppy wouldn't listen.

"She needs the experience and you need the help. No arguments."

"A thorn in my ass."

Poppy smiled, leaning up on her tiptoes to place a kiss on his cheek. She'd already told Arden to call her if they needed more help and Mack was being stubborn.

The two friends walked arm in arm toward the lodge.

"They're really back?" Poppy kept her voice lower than normal and it surprised Blair that she could still hear her.

"Yes." She mimicked the volume. "I've got a hacker working on a couple of things. One thing I know for sure is they haven't found who they're looking for. They wouldn't still be lurking if they had."

"I just don't see the connection to anyone here." Poppy shook her head.

"I know. But there is." Several connections. Poppy. The old bar she used to work at in the city. Whatever was in its safe. And Firebrook. A person living in Firebrook that worked at the school or attended programs at the library.

Blair's steps slowed. Poppy matched her pace, but didn't talk more. She knew when Blair had wheels spinning a mile a minute.

Blair had Sam looking at the employment records of the bar. If that connection didn't exist, then none of this made sense.

"You'll figure it out, Blair. You always do."

She did. But this was a little more personal. She'd thought it was personal because Poppy had been a target, but she realized it was the connection to Firebrook that made it personal. This place worked its way into her heart, claiming her as part of this home. She didn't like it being threatened any more than the people she loved.

People were already crowded around the fire pit. Caiden and Maggie stood close together at the barbeque. Blair wondered if locals told tourists it was a special event with the way they showed up, like it was an open party. But not a single person in the Greer family seemed to mind. Every guest was welcomed with a large smile and a plate full of food.

Noah worked next to his brother, gathering wood into small piles between the log benches and other seats.

It took less time than Blair thought it would for his head to snap up to meet her gaze. On the other side of the crowd, Wyatt did the same. In the next breath, they had two large bear shifters bearing down on them.

"We still haven't talked about you two mating." Poppy spoke with barely any movement to her lips.

"I'm not ready to talk about it."

"I remember a certain someone who forced me to talk about it."

"We know more now. I'm fine." Blair turned to her friend. "Really. I'm okay with it. We just have a few kinks to work out."

Poppy hugged her, but her mate pulled her away. She laughed and spun with him, trying to make him lose his balance. She had little luck.

"Hi, kitten." Noah moved in close, setting his hands against her hips and his nose to hers. He pulled her body against his, molding them together.

The tension from what happened still lurked. She saw something different in him. Surrounded by his family and in this setting, he was calm. Warm. Not that he was ever cold. But the warmth was different. It spread to his eyes and the tips of his fingers. This was where he belonged.

Blair would never be the person to tear him away from this.

"Hungry?" His question implied food, but the way he pressed his erection against her belly gave her ideas of something else she was hungry for.

He wrapped his hand around the back of her neck and took her mouth. Chaste, compared to the way he normally devoured her, but nonetheless strong.

These nights made his soul happy. With each year that passed, Noah felt the connection to home more.

As the night wore on, he saw that same connection wind its way around Blair. She fit in here. As if she'd been part of the family and community for decades.

People accepted her with her kind heart on display and wrapped in vines of protectiveness.

As usual, music played and people danced. Drinks were passed around and everyone had a great time. Tourists and locals were always the first to dwindle away, leaving the Greer family, and those they considered extended family, around the dimming fire.

Noah had separated his brother and two cousins from the group. "I want to go hunting tonight."

"Not alone."

"I will if I have to, but I know at least one of you will tag along."

"They'll want to come." Wyatt nodded at their mates huddled together with his sister.

"They can't." Blair would hate him for keeping her out of this, for diminishing her chances at finding answers, but Noah wanted these two gone. He wanted to extinguish the threat to his mate and his home.

"I know that." Wyatt shook his head.

"I'll stay with them." Tavis grudgingly volunteered.

"Blair won't enjoy being babysat." An image of her spitting curses at Henry from the cell made him grin.

"Neither will Poppy," Wyatt added.

"What do you suggest, then?" Tavis was clever enough to figure this out on his own, but somehow he wasn't quite catching on.

"Don't let them know you're babysitting." Noah shrugged.

"As soon as the fire's out." Wyatt walked away from them and toward Poppy.

"Wait." Tavis had a panicked look in his eyes. "They won't be in the same place to watch them, will they?"

"Nope." Noah sat on the log bench he'd sat on before with Blair, hoping to catch her eye and bring her over.

Her breath hitched, and she looked over her shoulder. Her cheeks were rosy from the few drinks she'd had and the heat from the flames. Standing, she made her way over to him, her tongue licking her bottom lip.

"I think I needed this." With only family around now, Blair set her knees on either side of his hips to straddle him rather than sit beside him.

"Oh?"

"Yeah. I get it, Noah. I'd never ask you to leave here. I don't want you to. I think it would destroy something inside you."

"You're right. It would. I don't like admitting that if it means we won't be together."

"I don't think that's what it means. It just means my future won't look quite like I imagined."

"And how does it look now?"

"I'm not giving up my job, and I travel a lot with my job. It will be more when I move here."

"When you move here?" Noah knew she had more to explain after that, but those words were the only ones that mattered to him.

Blair ran her nose down his, then tilted her head and took him in a rushed kiss. He held her hips against him and let her take as much as she wanted.

Several throats cleared around them in an obvious attempt to interrupt. Blair pulled away and glared at the others circling them. They all burst into laughter.

Then Tavis raised his beer. "Congratulations." The others followed his motion, murmuring their own felicitations.

They settled around the fire while the embers slowed. Noah didn't want to lie to Blair, but he knew it would be a battle to hunt down Scott and Luca.

"I think you should pack tonight."

"It's late. I can do it in the morning." Blair leaned her head on his shoulder.

"I'm an impatient man."

"I have a cure for that." Blair purred into his ear. That was the one thing that might make him hesitate. And also the one thing that would help him sneak out after. But he couldn't go that far.

"I know you do." He held her chin and kissed her, sliding his tongue along her lips. "Go pack, kitten. I'll be up soon." Noah attempted a look toward his cousins and brother that would make her think he had something to discuss alone.

"Fine." She sighed, cocking her head to Poppy, Maggie, and Dakota for them to follow. Tavis's job just got a little easier.

As soon as they were out of sight, Wyatt poured sand on the fire and they crept around the other side of the lodge.

"Just watch them. They don't need to know you're here. We'll be long gone before they realize what we're doing." Noah started stripping, piling his clothes under the bush with the others.

"I don't think any of you have as much faith in your women as you should." Tavis sauntered off toward the cabin, but kept his distance. They were all mated and had grown superior senses. Blair's were still developing. She had mentioned no changes to him, but that didn't mean they weren't happening.

Noah, Wyatt, and Caiden all pulled on the magic at the same time. Warmth filled him. There was an extra energy in the air with the three of them shifting at the same time. Minutes later, three similar looking grizzly bears stood together.

They stuck to the trees, but being so late at night, they didn't have to go deep. No one was out, so they had a little more freedom to make the hike to the other side of town quicker.

The scent trail was still there, thicker and harsher now that he smelled it with his bear's nose. Pungent enough to make him want to gag. The two clearly had nowhere to bathe.

I've got the centre. Wyatt, you take left and Caiden right. All of them worked for search and rescue. This wasn't their first hunt for people. However, it was rare they searched for the bad guys. A lawful search. This wasn't lawful.

Wyatt led the Search and Rescue team in Firebrook, but this was Noah's hunt, and neither of them questioned him.

They split up, their enormous paws stepping silently on the ground. The scent grew stronger the further he went. There wasn't anything up in these woods. Even the hiking trails split in other directions. This section of forest climbed the smaller foothills that sheltered Firebrook.

Old food sliced through the scent. His nose twitched as he found the discarded candy wrapper. As Noah had expected, they'd set up a camp. The more steps he took, the more garbage he found. The more the trail compacted against the ground.

Searching left and right, his sharpened eyes made out his two cousins closing in on the same area. They all paused, listening for voices, breathing, snoring.

Nothing.

Noah huffed out of his snout and closed in on the camp. It was a mess. And wouldn't be here for long with as much food as they'd left lying around. How had the wild bears living up not already ransacked everything?

They'd pegged a single tent to the ground between two trees, a tarp tied taut above it.

Where do you think they are? Caiden circled the camp.

Somewhere in town. Noah didn't think they'd get far in a search at night, unless they broke into the municipal office. *Let's see if we can pick up their trail going back.*

Popp, Maggie, and Dakota had gone home an hour ago, and there was still no sign of Noah. Blair walked down to the fire. Not a soul around, and the fire was out.

With her hands on her hips, she narrowed her eyes with the belief that it helped her to think.

That lying grizzly.

Poppy came over from the lodge. "Wyatt isn't inside."

"Noah didn't come to the cabin." It felt like she stated the obvious.

"And Caiden didn't come home." Maggie strolled down from the same path Blair had taken from the cabin. The trail leading to her house was across from the small cabin.

"They went hunting." Blair clenched her teeth.

"Then let's go." Poppy turned up the lane toward the woods.

"No. You two can't come." The point of Blair's mission had started with protecting her friend. She wouldn't allow her in the crosshairs again.

"As if we're letting you go after them alone." Poppy scoffed.

"You're not letting me. If we're spotted, I don't want either of you to become targets. Not just to keep you safe, but you'd be a distraction from what they're here for. It will take longer to figure it out. Especially you, Poppy. They might look at you as unfinished business."

"What about you?" Maggie squeezed her elbow.

"I'm only one little distraction. Besides, I don't intend on being seen."

"I can't let you go, Blair." Tavis appeared behind them. No one had heard him coming. Damn shifters and their silent feet.

A single look at Poppy was all Blair needed. With a battle cry, Poppy charged toward Tavis. "Get him, Maggie!"

Maggie, looking a little shocked, took a few seconds to catch on.

Tavis pulled, but he had a woman hanging on with all their weight on either arm.

"Thanks, guys. Have fun, Tavis." Blair called and bolted back up the lane for her car. Luckily, she'd taken her keys out of her purse and shoved them in her pocket. She maybe had a few minutes to get away from Tavis. Poppy and Maggie wouldn't be able to hold him back for long.

And she was right. As she drove down the lane, he stood in the middle with his arms crossed. Blair didn't like playing chicken.

"Get out of the car, Blair."

She shook her head and inched forward. Poppy and Maggie stood off to the side, unsure if they should get in the middle again. Sliding one hand to the window, Blair signaled to Poppy to pull Tavis to his right.

Counting down with her fingers—one, two, three—she waited for the two women to run at Tavis again.

But instead of moving out of their reach, he moved closer to her car.

Shit. She barely got the car in reverse before he laid a hand on the hood.

"We can stay like this all night until they get back."

Not happening. Blair backed up, kicking up the dust toward him. He chased her, clearly thinking the closer he was to the car, the less likely she'd try to get around him.

But while he still had his momentum, Blair cranked her wheel to angle the car, shoved it into drive and hit the gas.

Tavis's curse echoed behind her, cutting through Poppy's whoop.

Tavis would follow her in one form or another. At least he wouldn't lumber onto the street as a bear. But that didn't mean he wouldn't try to cut her off when she tried to follow Noah and the others.

Because, of course, he would assume she planned to follow Noah.

That was a stupid plan. And Blair wasn't stupid. She intended to set up her own stake out. Her best guess was that Scott and Luca had set up a camp of their own somewhere. And the only section of forest that didn't have hiking trails was in the foothills on the northwest of Firebrook. They had to have a preferred way to come in and out of town.

Blair parked her car in the middle of that neighborhood. It didn't matter if Tavis found it. She wouldn't be in it.

She ran around the houses and started walking just inside the edge of the trees. It took her half the time for her eyes to adjust to the dark. And even more surprising, the shapes of things were clearer. The mating changed her.

Nothing in the brush stood out. This line of trees was still too close to the houses. If Blair were sneaking in and out of town, this isn't where she'd do it. So where would she?

Lifting her head, she examined the neighborhood. There. The houses rounded a large corner, leaving more space between them and the trees. Fences sectioned off their properties and thicker growth blocked off the forest.

Blair ran past the houses until she reached the overgrowth. Then she kept her eyes peeled for any consistent tracks through it or around it.

There. Just around the edge. She followed the path to the trees to confirm. The path was clear for about ten yards. She'd found it.

Heading back to the thick bushes, Blair tucked herself into them several feet away from their worn path. And just in time for her to hear rushing feet over branches and debris.

"What is it with this place and fucking bears?" Panicked threaded Luca's voice.

"Shut up," Scott hissed.

Blair heard them, but couldn't see them. Their steps grew louder, but they weren't on the path they'd created. She didn't dare poke her head up any further to look around.

One of them crashed into her, his foot catching on her bent legs. He fell over her, his arms catching himself on the ground on the other side of her.

"What the fuck?" Scott rolled through the bush and weeds, shoving at the ground to stand.

"It's Blair." Luca stood behind her.

"You're a genius, Luca." She mumbled and pushed to stand.

"I don't think so." Scott had already stood and shoved his boot into her shoulder, sending her sprawling on the ground. Twigs scraped at her arms and face.

"Are you forgetting something, Scott? We don't have time for this."
Luca looked back at the trees. Noah and the others must have chased
them into town. This could have been a great plan if he'd included
her. Instead, it was a mess.

"They're gone, Luca. Calm down."

They stood too close for Blair to get herself in a position to trip
either of them. To do anything to them. She rolled, so she sat on her
butt, her knees bent to protect her centre as much as possible and her
hands ready to grab any feet they sent flying her way.

"You have a nasty habit of sticking your nose where it doesn't
belong." Scott sneered at her. "You're getting in the way."

"Scott." Luca tried to warn him again.

"Either shut the fuck up and help me or leave." Scott spit at Luca's
feet and shook his head. When he looked back down at Blair on the
ground, there was a sickening glee in his eyes.

This guy was seriously fucked up.

"Damn it, Scott." Luca cursed and reached down to grab her arm.
"We'll take her with us, then. We can't stand around here."

"You aren't taking me anywhere." She might find herself in a situation like this from time to time, but that didn't mean fear and panic
didn't surge through her when it happened.

Scott laughed. He lifted his fist, his aim true for her face. She
imagined he intended to knock her out. There was no way he thought
they could move her without her screaming and causing a scene. It
didn't matter that everyone had tucked themselves in their beds for
the night. In a town like Firebrook, everyone was nosy enough to get
out of bed to see what was going on. Just as they'd all rushed out when
she set off her car alarm. The news had spread down to Noah in only
minutes.

Blair's breath caught. They weren't alone anymore. She heard the
faintest huff of a breath.

Bad kitten. Noah's voice echoed through her. Seemed they had a connection during high emotional states. Like panic and fear. He wasn't happy with her. Well, she wasn't happy with him either.

Scott and Luca showed no sign of recognition. They didn't know that three gigantic bears were closing in. A circle of power, of energy, engulfed her.

"Hold her so I can knock her out."

Luca reached out for her hands where she held them in front of her face.

Three low growls erupted before he laid a hand on her. They froze.

"I told you so." Luca spoke through gritted teeth, his body unmoving in his half bent over position.

"I'm not through with you, Blair."

Chapter Fourteen

Noah had a mind to turn his mate's ass a beautiful shade of red soon. It took a hell of a lot of self control not to rip Scott to shreds. Wyatt had already warned him off when they broke through the trees.

Neither of them moved since the three bears let out their growls. They were frozen and bent over Blair, terrified to move and attract the attention of the bears.

"Or maybe I won't have to do anything about you. These bears can take care of you for me. Let's go, Luca."

"Go? Are you seriously thinking of running away right now?"

"I'm close to sending you the way of Mason if you don't grow some fucking brains and balls." Mason had been Poppy's ex and the third to the trio made with Scott and Luca. They'd murdered him when they'd been here in June. The reason was still part of the mystery. "Back away."

Scott inched backward, keeping his body bent. Luca walked around Blair to move away beside Scott. Wyatt was the closest and started stalking along with them. The thing was, they weren't wild bears. They wouldn't act like ones.

Caiden cocked his head as if interested in the movement and lumbered toward Blair, but when he reached her, he jumped over her. The quicker motion made both of them jump. They still hadn't made it out of the thick overgrowth.

As much as Noah wanted to add to their fear, he couldn't. Not with his mate still lying on the ground. Had they hurt her before they got there?

Hurry it up. He snapped at his cousins. Noah couldn't go to Blair with those two still near.

Wyatt and Caiden lunged a few times to startle them.

"Fuck." Scott cursed and gave up his careful escape. He grabbed Luca's arm and turned, running toward the closest house and weaving around it.

Noah rushed toward Blair, who still laid on the ground. Standing over her, he placed one paw on either side of her and brought his nose down to her face.

Whatever connection they had cut off once the panic in her receded. It was odd how they could communicate some times and not others.

"You *bearly* made it." She quirked her brows and braced herself on her elbows.

Noah growled, showing off his teeth. It wasn't the right time for bear puns.

Blair lifted one hand to run over his snout. At the last second, before she touched him, he snapped, clasping her hand between his teeth. He didn't bite, but he held her. She gasped and startled.

After several seconds, he released her hand and stepped back. She stood, but there was no caution or regret. His mate glared at him as if he'd done something wrong.

He had. He hadn't told her where they were going, but that wasn't as bad as her sticking herself in their path.

Noah bared his teeth the longer she continued to glare.

"No. You don't get to be mad. We're even. But this could have ended differently if you'd included me. Imagine what sort of trap we could have set as you three chased them out of the woods. I doubt they'll give us that opportunity again." Blair turned away from him, walking in the same direction as Scott and Luca.

Noah stomped in front of her.

"My car is that way."

Footsteps had all their heads turning. Tavis jogged toward them.

"Did you see them?" Blair pushed past him.

Tavis frowned. "No."

"Damn it." She looked over her shoulder and sent him another glare.

This woman was nothing but trouble. But she was his trouble.

She kept walking and Noah dashed forward to stop her again.

"I'm not leaving my car there."

"I'll walk her back." Tavis nodded at Noah. He had a frown trapped on his face. She owed him an apology. Not a promise to never do it again, but she didn't want him not to trust her in the future.

Noah grumbled as she walked away with Tavis.

She didn't speak until they got to her car. Both of them had their focus on the neighborhood. Scott and Luca should still be close.

Tavis's truck wasn't anywhere near. "Did you walk?"

"Sort of." Meaning he'd shifted and ran. He must have carried his clothes with him somehow.

"Get in." She pointed at the passenger side. But he was already reaching for the handle.

Blair pulled away, taking her time while still watching for any sign of them.

"I'm sorry." She glanced at him when she stopped at a stop sign.

"Oh?" His tone pitched up. Blair sighed. He was mad. Rightfully so.

"I'm sorry I had them attack you and that I ran."

"I'm not as hard and grumpy as my brother, but don't do it again."

"I can't promise that. This is my job."

"Chasing criminals isn't your job."

"You don't need to understand. But this is what I do. And I wasn't wrong. If Noah had included me, then tonight would have ended with those two in custody rather than in the wind again."

"Blair, mates are the most precious thing to us. Consider that the next time you chase criminals for the sake of a story." Tavis turned his head away, looking out the window. He wasn't angry that she'd run from him. He was angry on his brother's behalf. Because she put herself in danger.

He'd shut her out, but that never stopped Blair from saying what she wanted before. "That goes both ways."

His head turned the barest amount, but he still didn't look at her. Tavis could be mad, but ultimately, this didn't include him. This was between her and Noah.

She parked outside her cabin, but Tavis didn't get out. "Wait until he gets here."

Blair turned off her car and leaned her head back against the head-rest.

It didn't take them long. Noah and Caiden came around her cabin. Wyatt must have gone straight home to his apartment above the main lodge. Caiden kept walking past her car, heading toward the trail.

"Poppy and Maggie went home?" Blair asked Tavis before he got out.

"Yes." He looked at her. "You're family now, Blair. I don't want to see anything bad happen to you. It isn't just Noah that cares about you." Then he got out of the car.

Noah took his place. "My house."

Blair considered arguing. It was late, and they were already at her cabin. But his house was safer now that she was on Scott's radar.

Tension grew in her compact car. Thick enough she swore the metal seams were going to burst. At Noah's house, he met her at the front of the car.

He didn't give her a chance to say anything or to walk past him. Bending, he pressed his shoulder into her centre and lifted her.

Blair shrieked. "Put me down."

"Not a fucking chance, kitten."

Noah couldn't see straight. He should have included her. This would be over. Threat demolished. Instead, she took it into her own hands just as he had, putting herself in their path.

But knowing that didn't ease his ire. Ease the red hot emotions coiling tight around his veins.

At least the woman was smart enough to keep still as he slammed his front door and stormed to the bedroom.

"You have ten seconds to strip before I tear your clothes off you." Heat flashed in his eyes. His bear stalked close to the surface. Shifting back had taken longer. Caiden and Wyatt had looked on with worry in their eyes. With a roar, Noah had finished the painful shift.

"Noah. We need to talk."

"We can talk with my cock buried inside you. Eight. Seven. Six."

Blair tore her shirt over her head, but still had her shorts around her knees when he reached one. His growl started in his chest, but the vibrations reached all the way to his bones.

One harsh pull and she was free of her shorts. Magic pulse through his arm, he looked down at his hand. It was some half form with claws. Noah didn't waste the change. He tore through her bra and panties in seconds.

Blair let out a growl of her own, with gritted teeth and a snarl. Fucking adorable.

He pushed her back onto the bed. One hand gripped her knee, spreading her. No easing into it, no preparing her. He thrust in as his body covered hers.

She threw her head back into the pillow, giving him delicious access to her throat. He set his hand around it.

"What the hell were you thinking?" He punctuated his question with harsh thrusts. Their cores colliding.

She lowered her chin as far as his hand would allow. "I could ask you the same thing." She spoke as clearly as him. He hadn't tightened his hold around her neck. Yet.

"They aren't a threat to me. They are a threat to you."

"That was always the case. Tonight didn't change that." Her nails dug into his upper arms. The marks weren't permanent like his, but he'd wear them with pride all the same.

"Seconds, Blair. He was seconds away from knocking you out."

"You were there."

"But I might not have been." Every word they spoke came out with heightened frustration. They took it out on each other's bodies.

Noah pounded with full force. Blair dug her heels into his ass and tightened her fingers, cutting enough to draw blood. He smelled the copper as he moved over her. The tiny sting fueled this power between them.

"Nothing can happen to you. Nothing." Now he squeezed her throat. Just enough to make her react. Her eyes flared, but when he didn't squeeze further, Blair tilted her head again, leaning into his hold.

"The same goes for you."

Noah slammed into her and froze. "What did you say?"

"If I'm not allowed to put myself in danger, then neither are you. And don't tell me that hunting them down in the middle of the night didn't put you in danger."

"I will always put myself between you and danger."

"What a stressful life we're going to live."

"As long as we get to live it together."

Not a fucking thing solved, so Noah fucked her. He poured all of his emotion and fear into her. She submitted. Noah swore he felt hers in return.

The night hadn't gone as he'd planned. And it could have gone so much better.

Blair's hands moved to the back of his neck and pulled him down. She devoured his mouth as if her body was starved for him. He could relate. He was starved for her.

She bit his lip. Noah pulled away from her. She smiled up at him.

"Bad, kitten." He repeated his earlier reprimand. Blair licked her lips.

Pulling away from her, he gripped her hips and flipped her. She landed on her knees with her face buried in the pillow. Noah roughly rubbed his hand over her ass. As a test. Her breath hitched, and he watched her core pulse.

Perfect.

He brought his hand down on her ass, the sound echoing in the room and ringing in his ears. She pushed her ass back to meet him, so he did it again. And again. And again.

A sweet blush enveloped her skin. Noah wanted to do more, but he needed to be inside her more than that.

Pushing in, he pulled her back to meet his thrust. He wanted nothing about this to be gentle. Neither of them could handle gentle. They were angry. Noah was angry with her and himself. And scared. He needed to admit he'd been scared. Or that fear would forever rule their relationship.

What a stressful life we're going to live.

It ran like a warning.

But they couldn't compromise with his cock buried to the hilt in her heat and her walls trying to squeeze the life out of him.

Reaching around her, he pinched her clit.

"Come, kitten." The harsh command rumbled through his body. Her back bowed, and she pushed her hips further back. Not that there was anywhere for her to go.

Blair cried out and came around him. Noah didn't hold out. He let her pull him over, pumping into her frantically, imagining what his seed was doing.

They were one. They always would be.

Noah pulled back and rolled her over onto her back. Hazy eyes looked up at him. Still hard, he pushed back inside her. She whimpered.

"I don't know what to do with you."

Blair grinned. "You know exactly what to do."

"Brat." He kissed her nose. "I can't lose you, Blair. I was wrong not to talk to you first. But what were you doing there?"

"I found their path in and out of town. I was hiding to watch them come out. You three chased them and they must not have worried about finding their path. They charged through the overgrowth."

And tripped over her. Noah hadn't planned what to do after they found them at their camp. Tearing them to pieces wasn't a viable option. And Henry didn't know shifters existed. Sometimes it would be easier if he did. But none of them were comfortable with anyone knowing. No matter how much they trusted him.

"You're trouble."

"Tell me something I don't know."

"You're my trouble."

"I like the sound of that."

"Just..." Noah tried to find an acceptable compromise. "We'll both include the other in schemes from here on."

"I vow to do my best."

"Blair." Noah growled, burying his head into her neck and nipping the mating mark. She shivered. But that was the best he was going to get from her. He'd just have to be one step ahead of his mate.

* * *

Her body ached in the most devine way. As much as she would have liked to dwell in bed with that feeling, Noah had other plans.

He'd driven straight to the police station to tell Henry.

"I knew I should have kept you locked up." Although he'd mumbled it under his breath, he made sure he'd attempted to pin her in place with a look.

"He did it, too." Blair hiked her thumb over her shoulder at Noah.

"He did. I'm not happy about that either."

Noah shrugged. They'd given him the directions to their camp and the trail they were using in and out of town. She hoped Henry was smart enough to use the information to catch them rather than charge in and take over the spot, scaring them off or putting them further into hiding.

The next place they went was the cabin. Noah pulled out her suitcases and started throwing things in.

"Oh my God, Noah. Stop. I'll do it." Nothing was in any sort of sensible order. The girls had started to help her the night before, but they'd ended up in deep discussion about men and shifters. Most of it with Dakota covering her ears to block out certain details she didn't want to know about her brothers and cousins.

"Fine." He supervised her instead. The man stood there and watched every move she made.

"You don't have to watch. I'm moving in with you. Nothing's changed."

He closed his eyes and took a breath. His lips twitched as if he was choosing his words carefully. "Everything has changed for me."

"You're going to have to trust me."

He chuckled. "Never. You're going to get into more mischief every time I turn my back for years to come." His eyes softened. Seemed that wasn't a bad thing in his eyes. "I just don't want to let you out of my sight right now. You'll have to deal with it."

"I guess I should make sure you enjoy what you're looking at." Blair wiggled her brows, then twisted her body in a way that stuck her ass out toward him.

"Careful, kitten."

"Your warnings don't bother me."

His eyes dropped to her ass, but he didn't move. He let her finish packing undisturbed.

Shame.

As soon as Blair closed her suitcase, Noah took it out to his truck.

Blair would need to make some calls in the next few days. It would take some time to set herself up with work from here. But her podcast was the brunt of her work, and she could record anywhere. As long as she took frequent trips to the city, everything would work out. She hoped.

As if she'd brought the device to life, her phone buzzed in her pocket. Blair stopped on the small deck to answer. She smiled at the name. Sam didn't give her a chance to say hello.

"Gorgeous, gorgeous, gorgeous." Blair heard the tsk in his voice and imagined him shaking his head. "That was a lot of work and nothing interesting. You might need to make that two cakes you owe me."

"That depends. Two cakes is asking a lot." She leaned against the railing, catching Noah's eye as he walked back from the truck. "Nothing stood out?"

"Sorry, gorgeous. Nothing stood out, but that doesn't mean it isn't there. I'm sending you an email now with a list of employees from the last ten years."

"Any connections with the last three names I sent you?" Noah stood on the ground in front of her, listening to every word.

"None." He dropped the answer with confidence.

Blair sighed. "Thank you, Sam."

"Like I said, two cakes." She always bought him extra, but never two full cakes.

"Two teeny tiny cakes," Blair teased.

"Don't skimp gorgeous." Sam gasped with mock offense. "You'll hurt my soft little heart."

She snorted. There was nothing soft about him. "Bye, Sam."

"See you soon." He hung up and Blair put her phone back in her pocket.

"Who was that?"

"The confidential call I made the other day. A hacker friend. He's put together some information for me."

"You have a hacker friend?" He blinked up at her.

"Yes." Blair wrapped her arms around his shoulders. "A girl has to have resources."

Noah gave a noncommittal hum and she kissed the frown away from between his eyes.

He took her hand and led her off the deck and to the truck.

"I have some names to sift through."

"Want some help?" He shut her in the passenger seat of the truck, then hopped in the driver's side.

"That's sweet, but I'm okay doing it on my own. And you need to get to work."

The look he sent her made that sound like a low possibility.

"Noah, we both went behind each other's backs. It's over. Don't look at me like you can't trust me."

"Fine. I'll drop you off and leave you to unpack and get to work."

"Thank you."

True to his word, he helped her carry everything inside and left her alone. Blair felt safe in his home. Whereas at the cabin, she'd be easier to find if Scott came for her.

She forced herself to unpack her things. Unlike at the cabin, she had to unpack because there wasn't room for her suitcases. But Noah's house was spacious in comparison. She lived out of her suitcase when on the road.

But she wasn't on the road anymore. This was her home. It took time to break through that mental wall of unpacking, but she did it.

After storing her empty suitcase in the back of the closet, Blair grabbed her computer bag and set herself up at the small table.

She had coffee perking in the background and a bowl of chips beside her. This was going to take a while. Ten years worth of employees could be a lot of people. Some businesses always had lifetime people, those would be easier to rule out.

But the ones that only worked there for a few months? Any connection to one of them might be impossible to find.

Blair worked backwards through the list, starting with Poppy. Poppy had been their way inside, but if the person they were looking for had worked there when she did, they would have gone for them. Right?

The reason they were looking for them might change that theory.

One by one, she read the names. To herself and again aloud to help them stick somewhere in her memory. And read the time they'd worked there. The overlap between employees was complicated. Analyzing that wasn't necessary. Yet.

Her eyes had crossed by the time she got to the end of the list. Sam had been right. Nothing stood out.

Blair added the names of the two teachers and the secretary at the end of the list in case he missed something.

"You haven't moved much since I left, have you?"

Blair jumped. Noah stood on the other side of the table. She'd been so lost in the names, she hadn't heard him come in. "I have." She looked at the remnants of the snacks surrounding her.

"Find anything."

"No." She stretched, reaching her arms above her head and back. "But there must still be something missing."

Noah came closer, running his fingers over her cheek, then through her hair. "You'll figure it out." Leaning down, he kissed her.

The moment was a flash of their future. If kids ever became part of the picture, they might outgrow this house, but in the imaginary future, it was perfect. Blair looked forward to involving herself in the community. She looked forward to being near the family they had here.

She needed to make the call to her boss. It wouldn't be easy and they could deny her, laying her off instead of working with her to allow her to work remotely. They trusted her with her own podcast, but technically, they owned it. It was a call she dreaded. Ripping the bandage off always hurt, even if it was better in the end.

Blair had already fallen in love with Firebrook. Then she'd fallen in love with Noah. And now she fell in love with her future.

Noah straightened, but his eyes were different now. Warm and glowing, he stared down at her. Words weren't needed. He saw the same thing she did.

Chapter Fifteen

The next few days were quiet. Too quiet, if you asked Noah. Henry took his advice, and didn't charge into their camp, but he watched it, setting up cameras. He did the same along their path in and out of town.

Seemed the two had some intelligence if they moved camp. And they only moved it rather than leaving. Noah was sure of it. Scott had too much hatred the other night toward Blair to walk away. And if they hadn't walked away after getting caught in June and spending some time behind bars, someone potentially stumbling on their camp wouldn't do it.

But the lack of activity was eerie. The tension in the air rose like the temperature until the air was stifling. Like thick, suffocating humidity. But they didn't have much humidity here.

Every sound or smell grated on Noah's nerves.

Blair had reviewed the list sent by her hacker several times, and tried to find some connection to Firebrook by reading the names aloud to him. No one rang any bells.

Noah hated that he couldn't enjoy the first few days living with his mate. They were both always on edge, struggling to find comfort in this state of waiting.

He'd asked her about her job and how she planned to move herself here. She avoided the question.

And again the second time he asked. And the third.

He felt like a twisted bow string. Tavis had brought in Easton and Beck, one of the wolf shifters living outside of Firebrook, to help at *Rockhard*, effectively making Noah useless. Until this was over, he was.

"Blair." Noah cornered his mate in the kitchen while she poured her fifth cup of coffee that day.

"Yes?"

"We need to talk." He stood behind her, blocking her against the counter.

Her shoulders rose as she tensed. This was the point she'd cite an arranged coffee date with Poppy, Bonnie, or Maggie, and dash out the door. She didn't this time.

"You need to call your boss." Noah pulled in a breath. "Or you need to tell me you're leaving."

Blair spun around, knocking her full cup with her elbow. It poured across the counter, but she ignored it. "Leaving? What do you mean, leaving?"

"Going back. Not moving here."

"I'm sorry." Her eyes cleared. Pain seemed to make her nose scrunch.

The air left Noah. Not through his nose or mouth. It diminished from his body. No matter what happened next, he'd be devastated for the rest of his life. Either living without his mate or without his home.

"I'm sorry you thought that. I'm not leaving."

The words didn't register instantly, not with his sad future flashing before him. "Why are you avoiding your boss?"

"It will be better to talk to him in person."

That scared him just as much. People could be more appealing face-to-face.

"What is it?"

"Are you expecting difficulties from him?"

"I honestly don't know. I think that's one reason I'm digging in my heels."

"I'll feel better when you're fully moved in." Which wouldn't be until she finished her story about Scott and Luca.

Blair stood on her toes, reaching her arms around his neck. He still had his doubts. Trying to push them away didn't work. Time would ease his worries. Time with his mate in his arms.

"I love you, kitten."

"I love you, too." She kissed him. A soft press of her lips with an edge for more, but she pulled back. "I need to go bug Henry."

Noah started to offer to go with her, but she cut him off.

"Alone. Sorry, big bear, but you'll cramp my style. I'm not as irresistible with you standing beside me."

"Behave, Blair." The kiss he gave her wasn't as simple as hers. He needed to imprint himself on her before she left his sight, ensuring she'd be the first thing she'd think of before charging into danger.

"Oh, Henry! I'm back!" Blair singsonged her way into the police station. She heard the snickers from some of the officers and the secretary greeted her with an emphatic wave, then eagerly pointed her toward his office. "Thanks." Blair wiggled her eyebrows and saluted the other officers she passed. She enjoyed providing the entertainment.

When she opened his office door, he already had a harsh glare directed her way.

"Good morning. I spilled my coffee this morning so had to go out for a fresh one. And I thought to myself... Gee, I bet Henry could really use a coffee right now. So I got you one too." Blair set the cup in front of him. "Don't worry. I didn't do anything to it."

His hand froze in the air as he reached for it. Would serve him right if he thought so after locking her up.

Blair sipped hers while holding his gaze over the rim.

"I have nothing to give you, Blair."

"There's always something." She plopped down in the seat across from him.

"Nothing." Henry's voice rasped. Blair noticed his fists clenching on the desk. Frustration bled from him as fast as water running through a stream. Blair dropped her teasing.

"Okay. Take me through it."

"And give you ammunition to run off half cocked?" he shook his head and took the first sip of the coffee she brought him.

"I make no promises. But you need my help."

Several seconds of glaring back and forth and Henry caved. "I mean nothing. They haven't been back to their camp and they haven't used their path. They also haven't been on any footage since. Nothing has changed."

"Nothing only means that something is about to happen. We use the nothing to guess the something." But there was some information Henry didn't know. He didn't know that Scott had tripped over her and now wanted to get rid of her.

"Like what? Take more drastic measures to get inside the municipal offices?"

"Maybe. If they're looking for a person like we think, then that building is where all the records are. They're lying low. Something about the other night spooked them. If they haven't given up after everything went ass up in June, they won't give up now."

"This person must be important to them."

"Or to whoever sent them."

Henry straightened. "I hadn't considered they weren't the ones looking."

"That's something I've been wondering on and off. They aren't that bright." Blair tilted her head. "You know, you might consider making it easy for them to get inside the municipal offices."

"You mean set a trap?"

"Sure. An opportunity that's too good to pass up. Whatever it is, they're desperate enough to come back here. They haven't left." Blair didn't know that for sure, but it was in her gut. Instincts screamed at her that danger still lurked nearby.

"You're too smart for your own good."

"I'm amazing." A confident quirk of her brow cracked Henry's stern expression.

A loud knock echoed from the other side of the door. The person didn't wait for an invitation. A younger officer stepped inside. His lips clammed up when he saw her.

"What is it?" Henry didn't seem bothered by her presence anymore, despite all his determination that she should stay out of it until they were in custody.

"Clara is missing. She didn't show up for work and she isn't at home. Her sister is worried."

She and Henry shared a look. This was the something. It just wasn't what anyone would expect. Even Blair hadn't predicted something like this. It made little sense. Clara wasn't who they were looking for. They'd had multiple chances to take her before now without things getting as complicated as they have and getting caught the first time they were here.

Henry's eyes narrowed as he stood. If that look came from Noah, he might have pinned Blair to the chair. But Henry's warnings didn't bother her.

Blair stood, lifting her chin with determination. She recognized the fear trembling through Henry's hands, and those of the officer still at the door. They loved each and every citizen here. Small towns made things different with relationships. Blair knew that fear wouldn't affect their job.

"You either stay here or go home."

Blair tried a different tactic this time. Instead of being stubborn, she reached out and touched his arm. "I'm coming with you."

Henry didn't answer her, but he didn't stop her as she followed them out. Waiting in her car, she watched the patrol cars leave. Only then did she pull out behind them.

Blair expected them to block off the area around Clara's house, but they knocked on the door. They had to be sure she was missing.

"Clara. It's Henry Coates. Are you in there?"

Blair stood at the bottom of the cement stairs and listened, surprised she could hear so many little things. But none of them came from inside.

Henry knocked again and waited. When he tried the door, it opened effortlessly. It hadn't been locked.

The officers went first, ready with their hands hovering over their weapons. Blair slipped in behind them. He hadn't noticed right away, but when turning to view the whole living room, he froze when his eyes landed on her. His expression screamed, *What the hell are you doing in here?*

Blair waved her hands forward, telling him to carry on. If Scott and Luca took her, they didn't have time to worry about who was in the house.

She didn't believe they took her with the purpose of killing her, but she didn't think they'd let her live after the fact.

Blair didn't understand their purpose in taking her, though.

The house looked immaculate. Clara was a tidy person. Minimalistic, but she had full shelves. Books, plants, trinkets. She cherished the things that were important to her. All of those things were in plain sight.

Cushions were perfectly straight on the furniture. Blankets folded neatly over the back. This woman was a cozy creature.

Henry and the others had split up through the house. Blair took more time to look over individual items. Something was off, yet everything was perfect.

She spun in a circle as Henry moved down a hall. A corner of a piece of paper stuck out from behind the stand by the front door. Moving closer, she saw it was an envelope with a name written on the front. The last thing Blair wanted to do was touch potential evidence. Leaning closer to the wall, she tried to see the name without pulling it out from behind the succulent.

They'd scrawled her name across the front in a messy scratch that she was sad to say she recognized.

A quick glance over her shoulder said she was still alone. Grabbing the envelope, she shoved it in her back pocket.

"Find something?" Henry came back into the living room.

"No. Nothing." She'd show him after she read the letter for herself. Then they could come up with a plan together. With Noah, too. But this was bait specifically meant for her.

"Nothing is out of order. It's possible she's out doing something she didn't tell anyone about. I can't say for certain she's missing."

"You don't believe that any more than I do."

"No."

The envelope burned in her back pocket. She needed to read it. She should show it to Henry.

Sighing, Blair let her gaze drop to the floor.

"Henry." She crouched down. "It is out of order. Look" She pointed to the scrapes on the floor just behind the couch.

Henry crouched down beside her. "That could be old."

"It's not." Blair ran her finger over the tiny shavings from the wood flooring. "Look for more things like this. There was a struggle, but they put it all back together. She has so many things on her shelves and tables. There's no way they got everything perfect."

"Right. Dust circles, discolouration."

"Exactly." Blair helped find the first few signs before slipping out of the house. No one noticed she'd left.

In her car, she pulled the note from her back pocket and tore it open.

The words read like a sick poem. Her blood ran cold and her heart hammered to compensate.

Blair tossed the note out of her car window and drove away before it floated to the ground. She didn't have enough time.

I ce pierced through Noah's chest. It was momentary. Came and went in a flash with his heart pumping wildly to rid his body of the torment.

When Blair left to talk to Henry, he'd gone to work. Tavis and the others had the customers taken care of, so he'd stayed in the main office going over their schedule for the rest of the summer. He'd blocked off some time to go with Blair to pack her apartment in the city.

Noah tried to ignore the discomfort, but it left a trail. A scar. This wasn't just any instinctive reaction. Something was wrong with Blair.

His phone buzzed in his pocket, and he dreaded answering it. Wyatt's name flashed on the screen.

"What happened?" Noah didn't need to contemplate the ice piercing pain or the incessant scar left by it.

"Clara is missing. Henry just called. He wants us to be ready for a search and rescue."

Not Blair. Noah attempted a breath, but his lungs wouldn't cooperate. "Be ready?"

"He doesn't know where to look. He thinks she's been taken, but they've covered their tracks well. We have nothing to start with."

"Where's Blair?" She'd been with Henry this morning.

"She's not with you?" Wyatt didn't sound concerned. Noah tried to pull on that for comfort. But he'd gotten to know his mate pretty well. And when she'd promised not to chase danger, she'd been lying. They both knew it, and Noah hadn't called her on it.

"No, she went to talk to Henry this morning."

"He said nothing about her." Wyatt's tone held a shrug.

Noah's throat constricted. But the feeling came through on a connection. Not his own body's reaction. Panic filled him as if he'd become a great empty chasm, yearning to be fed.

What have you done, kitten?

Noah hung up and shoved his phone back in his pocket. Gravel kicked up behind him as he drove off toward Clara's house. The most likely place to find Henry. And he hoped his mate. But in that panic filled chasm, he knew better.

They'd taped off the house leading to the door, but they hadn't bothered with anything further than that. Henry stood outside, talking with the other officers and with his face veiled with fury. The man was pissed. He cared about the people here and always showed a little more emotion than others.

Wyatt pulled up behind Noah only seconds later, but Noah was already out of his truck and on his way toward Henry.

"Where's Blair?" Noah called out.

Henry's head whipped around so fast, Noah wondered if he'd crack his neck. "I can't find her." He spoke through his teeth. "Her car is gone." Noah followed Henry's glance to an empty space next to his car.

Noah pulled out his phone.

"Don't bother. She isn't answering." Not only was Henry pissed, he was worried about Blair. Noah heard it in his voice, saw it in his eyes and the pinch of his lips.

Panic reclaimed Noah's body, but this time his own. He strolled over to the empty spot, hoping that just imagining her here would give him insight to where she'd gone.

But he may have found something better. A folded piece of paper lay on the ground, the breeze gently moving it. He picked it up and unfolded it.

* * *

An exchange, Blair.
You for her.
Everything you have in that head of yours doesn't need out.
Northwest for six kilometres.
Then North for two more.
Over the cliff you go, and up the cliff she'll come.
One o'clock.
Better run.

* * *

She would. Blair would run off to rescue someone without a thought of a coordinated plan. Especially with a time constraint. But she left the note. A clue of her own for them to follow.

He read the note again, because the first time was pure torture and he hadn't processed more information than his mate was in danger. It read as if Scott enjoyed writing it. But more than that, the intent behind it was loud and clear. A trap for Blair, but they wouldn't let either of the women go.

Wyatt appeared over his shoulder. The familial presence did nothing to calm him.

"Fuck." His cousin cursed after taking a moment to read the note. Noah read through the directions he'd given her. They were vague, but direct. He tried to remember what was up there. What cliff could be there?

Large, harsh and jagged, with several outcroppings for stopping points, but they weren't big. And as time had worn on, not all of them were stable. At the bottom was the Huntington river—large, deep, and held the bottom portion of that cliff along the bank.

It would be a miracle for even a shifter to survive that fall.

Noah met his cousin's eyes. They had to hurry. Wyatt glanced at Henry. They didn't have time to go through the process to send people out there. This wasn't only for the search and rescue volunteers. Henry wouldn't allow them to lead the way and put civilians at risk.

He shook his head and motioned for Wyatt to get back in his truck. Noah would let Henry know where so he could come deal with Scott and Luca—or the bodies of Scott and Luca. But not until they were ready to shift and sprint through the woods giving them a head start.

Noah didn't have the brain function to call his own brother, and he trusted Wyatt understood that, having been through a similar situation with Poppy. Wyatt would call Tavis and Caiden. Maybe more.

Images of his mate's broken and torn body blacked out the drive outside of town. The drive there felt more like an old, faded memory. His heart went between beating too slow, barely enough to keep him alive, and beating too fast, trying to kill him with panic.

He refused to lose her. His heart needed to get itself under control.

Chapter Sixteen

Her legs burned. Fire coursed through her muscles until all that was left was charred, brittle coal. But Blair kept going. Of course, the asshole chose a large incline to hike up. Must be a fucking tall cliff she was about to jump off. She crossed her fingers more than once that deep, smooth water coated the bottom to land in rather than sharp, jagged rocks. It was a fool's hope, but she let the flames beating through her body feed it.

Blair had a hiking go-bag in her car. She always did, but before coming to Firebrook, she restocked it and added a few things. One being a GPS. She reached the six kilometres about ten minutes ago. Two more wouldn't take long if her body wasn't begging her to stop for a rest. Blair refused to even stop for water, manhandling her bag to pull out her bottle while still moving.

She had little chance of sneaking up on them, of looking before approaching. No plan, no hope of outsmarting them. The only hope was that someone would find the note. Preferably Noah.

They'd linked in times of panic before. Blair tried to use it. Yelling, whispering, thinking. Squeezing her eyes shut and picturing his face. Nothing. Which only increased her fear.

This would end in one of two ways, and there was nothing more Blair could do. Stall them maybe. But at least she'd save someone in the process. Someone who didn't deserve to be dragged into the middle of God knew what.

And that's what nagged at Blair the most, despite her upcoming fall off a cliff. Not knowing what these two wanted. That mystery became an incessant nag at the base of her skull. But it was Noah and the life they'd only had a taste of that hurt. Losing that fed the most excruciating pain she could imagine. Acknowledging that thought would turn her feet into cement blocks and stop her in her tracks, condemning an innocent woman.

"Seems you're more predictable than I thought." Scott's voice startled her out of her pain and fueled the panic. She hadn't been looking ahead of her. With this being the last stretch of her destination, she'd focused on forcing her body to move through the exhaustion and the emotions.

Blair panted, hoping her burning lungs weren't the last thing she ever felt in this life. She shrugged and huffed out, "There's still time."

"Not much," Scott said with a smirk. Luca stood a short distance behind him, leaning against the tree and as he had with everything these two had done together, he looked a little uncertain.

"Where is she?" Blair stopped. His voice indicated the end of her destination, and her body refused to take another step.

Scott's sickly disturbing grin didn't change as he tilted his head to his right. The incline continued a short bit, but came to an abrupt stop. A rope curved over the edge, pulled tight from both ends. Blair followed the line of the rope. They tied it around the base of the tree at Luca's feet.

"Can't use your big boy words, Scott?" Every fibre in her body pulled as tight as that rope to keep her from going to the edge of the cliff.

"You won't be so snarky on your way down." He bent and pulled another rope up from the ground behind him. He tossed the end through the air to land in front of her. "Tie it around yourself. Hope for your sake you were a girl scout. Or did you only sell cookies?"

His question didn't require an answer. She may not have been a girl scout, but she'd learned some basic knots on her own and a few from Noah on his climbing lessons. As long as she did it correctly, it'd hold her until someone found her. At least her end would hold. She didn't trust the knot Scott was tying around the tree closest to him.

"Off you go."

"Bring her up, first."

"Didn't you read the note? Down you go. Up she comes."

This was happening too fast. Blair's mind whirled, gripping onto so many possibilities. The end of her life. The end of Noah's. Clara's family. Would Noah ever forgive her for coming here without telling him? She should have told him. Their goal had been her. She'd had enough time to organize help to save Clara. But Blair hadn't risked it. If it was Luca calling the shots, then maybe. But Scott was cruel.

She needed to stall. There might not have been enough time for Noah or anyone to find the note and find her. They may never find her.

"Why are you doing this?"

"You're a pain in the ass."

"You're not going to let me hang there, are you?"

He only grinned.

"If that's how it's going to be, then tell me what you're looking for. Who you're looking for."

"Not a fucking chance. That never ends well for the villains in the movies. Spill their guts before they gut the witness, then the tables turn. My lips are sealed."

"Luca." The more this went on, the more Blair wondered if Luca would give up whatever this was. Luca didn't have the stomach for this like Scott, but he went along with it all, anyway. It made her wonder if the original job had nothing to do with murder.

"He's not saying anything either." Scott answered, but Blair didn't let her gaze wander from Luca. He couldn't meet her eyes. His jaw clenched, and he looked away.

"You don't have to go along with him, Luca. It will be two against one. We could stop him together." Blair swore Luca took a step toward them. Maybe her hope imagined things.

"Shut up! Get over the edge before I shove you over." Scott lunged. It startled her enough to make her move, and once she did, he stopped.

Unshed tears blurred her vision with each slow step toward the edge. With a few more steps to go, she leaned forward, stretching her body to look over the edge. Clara clung onto the rope tied around her waist, her head bowed against it. The ledge on the cliff was barely big enough for her toes. Her body shook violently with the effort to hold herself there.

"Pull her up as I go down."

"You don't make the orders."

Blair looked at Luca again, hoping he'd at least honour this much to free her. She accepted there may not be a chance at freedom for her, but there had to be for Clara.

"Move," Scott snapped.

Blair wanted to call out to her, to reassure her, but she didn't think there was any reassurance. That wasn't a promise she could keep, either.

Controlling her trembling body, Blair turned around and started threading the rope through her hands to pull it tight from the tree. This wasn't the sort of climbing that Noah had taught her, but she prayed the same basics applied.

Backing up, she felt for the edge of the cliff with her foot. As her stomach bottomed out, she pushed her feet against the edge and leaned her weight back. The scream she tried to hold back came out of her, muted and strangled, but a high sound nonetheless.

"Blair?" Clara's voice didn't sound like hers, but she didn't imagine many sounded like themselves when terrified for their life.

Blair glanced down to see her looking up at her and that initial flash in her eyes was hope. Hope of a savior, but Blair wasn't going to save her. Only be her companion. She'd known it was a trap, but she'd foolishly thought she'd save Clara. The look in Scott's eyes banished that idea.

Rappelling was hard and terrifying. A constant feeling of falling every time she moved further down, but that was more due to the circumstances rather than the activity.

"Keep going until there's no more rope." Scott leaned over the top, a disturbing gleam in his eyes.

Blair's rope let her go a little further than Clara, and she was lucky enough to find a tiny lip to brace her feet, but she had to stretch to take any of her weight.

"Someone is coming, right?" The wind carried over Clara's murmured words and guilt punched Blair in the gut.

"I don't know." But she should. Tilting her head back, she yelled up at Scott sitting on the edge, swinging his legs like a child on a playground. "Pull her up and let her go. Now."

"No. But I'm going to have a bit of fun before I cut the ropes."

As a group, four grizzlies ran, weaving around trees and cutting a straight line to the cliff. The energy of the shifters, of his family, pushed Noah forward. Pushing him to keep his sanity to save his mate.

The cliff was in range. The putrid scents of Scott and Luca curled his nose. Tavis cut in front of him.

Charging in could put them in more danger. We need to slow down and sneak in.

Noah snarled at his brother. He didn't want to wait; he didn't want to plan. He wanted to shred them to pieces. It didn't matter that Tavis was right.

We should spread out and surround them. They'll have nowhere to go with the cliff. Tavis spoke with clarity.

Sure they do. They could go over the cliff. Noah wouldn't try to stop the assholes, either. Death from the rocks or death from the bears. Hell of a choice to make.

Wyatt and Caiden chuffed with agreement.

You all forget that Henry is right behind us.

Less mess for him to clean up, Caiden suggested.

This is wasting time. Noah pushed past his brother and lumbered steadily through the trees. He didn't care what the others did, but they had to follow him and adjust whatever plan they wanted according to him.

He had full intentions of sneaking in and taking them out. But yelps and screams filled his ears and thinned his blood. One of them was Blair. It didn't matter what state she was in, he'd recognize the range of her voice.

Blair! He yelled after her, not knowing if she heard him. He heard nothing other than her fear. It had a voice of its own. Terrifying pain throughout her whole body reverberated into his.

"Scott, stop it. This isn't part of the job." Luca growled. At least he wouldn't fight back when they attacked. Noah's sole focus trained on Scott.

"Leave, Luca. If you don't want to have fun, there's no need for you to spoil mine." Another yelp followed Scott's words. It wasn't Blair's, but it enraged Noah all the same. He felt the others around him. They'd spread out to attack from all sides. Once the cliff edge came into view, Noah didn't give a shit what they did.

Luca paced back and forth, running his hands through his hair. Scott sat on the edge of the cliff, tossing rocks over on each side of him and shaking the two ropes pulled tight. He was fucking tormenting them.

Noah saw an easy way to end this. It wouldn't take much of a push to rid the world of that garbage.

"Scott." Luca straightened and his voice trembled. He'd caught sight of them. Noah let his lips curl into a sneer, but didn't hold Luca's gaze. He watched Scott and knew if he intended to charge, he had to do it now. Scott wasn't listening to Luca, but the warning was coming.

"Fuck off, Luca." Scott snarled over his shoulder, and as he took in Luca's expression and dead stare, he whirled around.

"Bears." Luca's warning came out as a choked whisper.

Scott scrambled up from the edge of the cliff and Noah's opportunity slipped away. Oh well, there were other ways to get him over the edge to his death. So the scum couldn't come back again.

Caiden was closest on Noah's right, closing in on Luca. Slower than a crawl, intimidating with every step. Wyatt was next, eying the ropes. Noah's sights were on Scott.

If you can hear me, Blair. We're here.

He didn't get a response. The panic between them was loud enough he barely heard himself.

Tavis stalked closer to the cliff's edge.

Luca was done. Noah recognized the failure in his eyes. He doubted this man would be a problem after this. His feet inched backward while his eyes darted from bear to bear. With his head shaking, he took large steps, but still moved so as not to startle the large wild predators bearing down on them.

Scott wasn't as smart. His focus was on the ropes. He watched the bears, but his gaze drew to the ropes more than them.

Reaching behind his back, he held onto something before pulling it free.

"You're a fucking idiot." Shocked fear spat from Luca, and he quickened his steps. Caiden continued to close in on him, but knowing he wasn't the highest threat, didn't attack.

Decisions played across Scott's eyes like a reel. Nostrils flared, he let his attention drop on the ropes. From one to the other and back. Noah didn't know which rope held which woman, but he scented them both. Their fear and sweat floated up in strong drafts from the wind that climbed up the cliff from the water. But whichever Scott decided on would be Blair's. Clara had been the trap. Scott had it out for Blair—it would be her he'd eliminate first.

It all happened so fast. Scott pulled the knife from behind him and dropped to the ground. The blade sliced through the rope with only a little resistance. Only enough time for Tavis to latch his jaw around it.

The force of the release launched Tavis closer to the edge. His claws made large divots in the ground as he braced himself to keep from going over the edge. Blair screamed, the sound long with piercing painful pitches where he imagined she jerked against the rocks.

"Blair!" Clara called out over the commotion, her own fear and pain scratching her voice.

Scott hesitated over the other rope, but Wyatt was already there, ready to grab it. Noah only saw one thing, a bright, incessant target on Scott's chest.

He charged, coming up on his hind legs at the last second to swat him down to the ground with his paw. Noah's claws curled around Scott's throat. He felt his pulse triple and smelled urine as the piece of shit understood the danger he was in and that he wouldn't live a minute more.

Noah! Tavis grunted, strain evident through the connection.

The ropes are weak, Noah. Wyatt's warning almost made it through.

But it was Caiden charging back toward him that tore his focus. He shoved Noah off of Scott and took his place only long enough to knock him out with a solid hit. *Killing takes time we don't have.*

Noah looked at Tavis holding the rope. Wyatt wavered between the two, wanting to help Tavis, but guarding the other rope.

Fuck. The ropes wouldn't last much longer.

Tavis had come in with a pack of climbing gear and clothes. Knowing that Henry would be behind them, they wouldn't want to expose themselves. He must have dropped the pack before Luca spotted them.

Noah saw it about ten feet behind Tavis and shifted while rushing toward it. Caiden shifted with him.

They slipped on pants first and had themselves geared up only a minute later. There was no need to speak. Each knew what they had to do. Noah was getting his mate and Caiden would get Clara.

Wyatt glanced over the edge and shook his big head. Noah could only focus on one thing at a time or he'd fuck this up. He'd never felt such fear in his life.

She felt Noah, heard him in her mind in the distance, but Blair hadn't been able to grasp onto the connection. She used all her strength on the rope.

The knot around her waist slipped and the only thing keeping it from completely unraveling was her arms pulling her up. Just that inch. She'd had a decent grip, albeit shaky, until the rope broke. Or it was cut. Something changed up there and made Scott move away from the edge. That something being her mate.

Her hold had slipped as she'd dropped two feet, then lurched to a stop. She had nowhere for her feet. Those small outcroppings were several feet away from her and the surface near her feet was all smooth. Everything in her burned and her muscles trembled as she continued to lose strength.

Watching her death approach scared her now that she was over the edge. It wouldn't be sudden, nor quick and painless. The water and rocks would rush at her and she'd never know what she'd hit first, or what lay beneath the surface of the water. Blair imagined more rocks, just as sharp and jagged at the rest of the cliff.

She'd adopted the same position Clara had when she lowered herself. Head bowed against her hands on the rope, but now her hands gripped above her head. Her eyes had opened momentarily when she fell, but she'd since closed them tighter than before.

Blair held onto some of her bravery for most of this. The more Scott chipped away at them, the more fear of falling grew. She was an uncontrollable mess now.

"Blair." Noah's voice didn't sound so distant anymore. But she couldn't make herself look.

She plummeted another inch. Her stomach lurched, and she screamed.

"I've almost got her, Tavis! Hold on!" Noah was closer now. Tavis must have been the one who caught the rope.

Blair let her head rise and only opened her eyes to slits. She didn't want to see anything other than Noah. He was there, but not within reach.

"N... No.. Noah." Tears spilled, and she shut her eyes against the emotions in his. She didn't want his fear reflected at her to be the last thing she saw when she fell. Pulling on the sweetest memories of their time together, she let them play in her mind.

"I'm coming, Blair."

"I love you, Noah. And I'm so, so sorry."

"Tell me at the top, kitten."

The rope slid another inch. Her scream came out strangled this time. Panic bouncing around off the rock face. Hers. Noah's. Clara's.

His arm around her waist made her jolt. Closer to him, but the sudden motion of her body pulled too much on the rope. Noah tried to grab her. His arm tightened, but she still slipped. It was a scramble to grab onto him, but her muscles refused to work anymore.

"Blair!"

She screamed again as she fell out of his arm. Noah pushed off the cliff and swung himself closer as he moved down. Not as fast as her, but fast enough to grab the rope. It tightened around her waist, stopping the knot from pulling all the way free. Sobs racked her as she retook her hold on the rope. It wasn't enough. She carried little of her own weight.

Noah had one hand on his rope and one on hers. He had no way to adjust to pull her up.

"I'm coming down!" She couldn't tell who yelled over the edge.

"I'm sorry. I'm so sorry, Noah."

"Not now, Blair. We're getting to the top. There's no other option, mate."

Blair pulled on his confidence and put it into her muscles. She only had to hold on a little longer. And not jerk at someone's touch this time. Just hold and stay still, those were her only jobs.

The rope moved, and she looked. Wyatt was there, taking the rope from Noah so he could lower further down the cliff.

"Don't move, kitten." His feet were level with her hands. "Just a little further." Two feet out of reach. "We won't let you fall." His arm crept around her waist.

Her lungs seized and her body twitched with his touch, but she kept herself as still as possible.

"That's it, Blair. I've got you." This time, he tightened his arm around her and pulled her close. "Wrap your arms around my neck."

"I'm too weak to hold on."

"I know. I've got you." He moved something from his waist. "Legs up too."

He wrapped something around her bottom and her waist. A type of harness, she assumed. It didn't hold all of her weight, but it helped. Blair did her best to hold on to Noah.

"We're going to move now."

She appreciated the warning. Burying her face in his neck, she waited while they rose. Every few steps, he set his hand on her bottom and hips, pulling her against him a little tighter.

"We're at the top. I need to pass you up."

"No. I can't move."

"Then don't. Just stay still and let go of me. Wyatt, Caiden, and Tavis are all right here. They'll take you." Noah's voice soothed. He was calm and strong and everything she needed to be and wasn't. Blair would readily admit that this experience was too much.

Hands grabbed her under each shoulder and pulled. She whimpered as the space widened between her and Noah.

"It's okay, Blair." Tavis spoke near her ear. Soon an arm banded around her from behind and pulled her onto solid ground. By the time she opened her eyes, Noah cleared the edge. But she couldn't move.

He didn't bother taking the harness off him. He only detached the rope and fell to his knees in front of her. Lifting her at her hips, he crushed her to him.

"Fuck, kitten."

No words formed, only sobs. Body wrecking sobs as Noah moved them so she sat on his lap and buried against his bare chest.

His hands ran up and down her back, soothing murmurs came from his lips. Blair lost all track of who and what was around her. Time passed in his arms and that was all she needed.

"I'm sorry. I'm sorry." The words were a fervent litany.

"I know, kitten. It's okay. You're both safe." That brought her head up. She blinked several times to clear her vision. Caiden sat with Clara several feet away as she still looked shocked with tear-stained cheeks. He wrapped an arm around her shoulders, rocking her.

"Where are they?" She couldn't see anyone other than Clara and the Greer men.

"Luca ran off, Scott is unconscious and tied up in that direction." Wyatt stood against a tree, keeping watch over everyone.

Tavis knelt down beside them. "You okay?"

"No." She was safe. But she wasn't okay. She was far from okay.

He nodded, then looked at Noah. "Henry is close. I had nothing more than pants and climbing gear packed in the bag."

"It isn't the first time he's found us like this. His focus won't be on us. We'll deal with his questions later." Wyatt pushed off from the tree and started hiking back down the hill, presumably to meet up with Henry.

Henry was going to be livid with her. And Blair found it hard to bear the disappointment. From Noah, from Tavis, from herself, and from Henry. She knew it was coming.

"I think Wyatt is a little too calm. Henry will want answers about us some day. It's arrogant to think we'll never have to let him in on our secret." Tavis stood and stared after his cousin.

"You're probably right. But we'll cross that bridge another time. Right now, I'm not moving." Noah's arms tightened around her. And that was the only thing Blair needed. Her mate.

Chapter Seventeen

N oah kept his hand on the back of Blair's head, holding her against his chest and massaging his fingers into her scalp. She wasn't asleep, but neither was she in full consciousness. The shock still gripped her tight, but his mate eventually calmed in his arms.

Listening to her heartbeat, feeling her heat and pulse satisfied the animal still raging against his ribs. He wasn't sure when he'd ever settle. Anger, fear, hope, and love were having a war of their own in his head. He was angry with his mate, and Noah didn't like that.

They'd both known her promise to stay out of danger had been empty. This was as much his fault as it was hers. But she still ran head first into this without at least making a phone call. Precious minutes had been lost. Her remorse was painful, even for him. Whatever bond they had as mates was clear of all disruptions now. No fear or panic distorted the signal.

Regret hurt.

Henry stomped through the woods ahead of Wyatt. Face red with rage and eyes accusing every single one of them for working without him. The four of them did the same thing to Henry as Blair had to Noah. A chain of bad decisions made with the right intentions.

Noah continued to hold Blair. She was oblivious to the new presence, which suited him fine for the moment.

Henry spotted them on the ground and started their way. Noah gave an imperceptible shake of his head. Locking his jaw, he halted. Wyatt stepped up beside him and pointed to his right where they'd tied up Scott.

Caiden still stayed close to Clara. She needed the support as much as Blair.

Noah was loath to move, to disturb Blair. But he didn't want her to come to her senses with Henry bearing down on her.

Taking several deep breaths, he closed his eyes and tried to lend her his strength. Holding her, cradling her, stroking her—Noah hid his anger from the day.

He listened to Wyatt and Henry talking a distance away. When Wyatt approached the end of his altered series of events, Noah bent his head to speak in Blair's ear.

"Time to move, kitten." He gently squeezed the back of her neck, sparking sensations in her body.

"Moving brings nothing good."

"Sure it does. Maybe not right away, but once we move, I can take you home. Four walls, a floor, and a bed."

She nuzzled her cheek against him and felt wetness. Her tears resurfaced. "Noah..."

"Not now, Blair. I know what you want to say. I can feel it. I have things I want to say too. But not now, not here."

She looked up at him, separating them the first inch.

"Henry is here."

Blair's eyes widened and her face paled further than the shock caused. "He's going to hate me."

"No. Angry? Most definitely. But that man won't hate you." He stroked the back of his knuckles over her cheek.

"Noah has it right." Henry came around the tree they were leaning against. "I don't hate you, Miss Marshall. I'm in awe of your bravery to save Clara. But I'm angry as hell you didn't show me the note and ran off. Don't expect my trust to come so easily next time."

Blair's jaw clenched at the dressing down and her eyes filled. Noah wanted to beat Henry, but he should beat himself afterward. The officer's words mirrored his own he needed to get through to his mate.

Henry crouched down beside them and set his hand on Blair's shoulder. "I'm happy you're safe, Blair." The friendship the two of them seemed to develop over this chase shone in their eyes as they looked at each other.

Blair had a way of getting under people's skin. In a good way. She'd wormed her way into this community as if she'd intended to stay all along.

"I need statements. As soon as possible. I know you likely want to go home, but that will have to wait a bit longer. I'll be back when I'm finished talking to Clara." Henry stood and walked around to Caiden and Clara. Caiden still stayed near, able to listen to what she recounted that could affect them.

They waited, adjusting on the ground to bring blood flow back into their bodies. Blair's muscles still hadn't recovered, but she regained enough strength to sit on her own beside him. Noah left the cleaning up of the gear to Tavis and Wyatt.

When Henry finished with Clara, Caiden escorted her to the side-by-sides brought in by the other officers to be taken back to town. He offered to go with her, but she refused. Colour seeped back into her cheeks. After a piercing look, Caiden nodded and let her go back alone with one of the officers. Three others already took Scott back half an hour ago. Thankfully, still unconscious.

As Henry came back to them, the only ones left were the four shifters wearing only jeans. Barefoot and bare-chested. Three of them standing like guards in a semi-circle around Noah, Blair, and Henry.

Henry frowned at them before sitting on one knee next to Blair.

"Let's hear it. What happened?"

"I'm so sorry, Henry." She choked up again, but clamped her lips shut, swallowing it down.

Henry sighed. "I know. Let's move past that. What happened? Where did you find that note?"

"On an end table near Clara's front door. It had my name on the front. I hid it until you were occupied elsewhere, then I left and read it in my car."

"Why didn't you show me right away?"

"I didn't plan to run off. I wanted to read it myself before you took over."

"You were planning to come inside and show me?"

"Yes. But..."

"He gave you an ultimatum with a time limit."

Blair nodded. "I had to go. I tossed the note out the window, hoping someone would find it soon, and I left. I didn't stop—not for a breath and not for a break. Not until I reached here."

"Okay. And what happened when you got here?"

"I tried to see if he'd talk. He wouldn't. Luca tried to convince him to stop, saying this wasn't part of the original job, but Scott wouldn't listen. He tossed me the rope, made me tie it around myself while he tied it around the tree. He made me climb down over the edge. Then sat there." She eyed the edge of the cliff. "Throwing rocks at us and shaking the ropes."

"What did you hear between that and when these guys climbed down to get you?"

"Nothing. My ears rang deafeningly with fear and panic."

True enough. Blair hadn't known they'd been there. Noah hadn't been able to get through to her.

"Okay. You didn't hear anything. But what else happened in that time?" Noah didn't miss the looks Henry made toward the deep claw marks in the ground where Blair had hung.

"The rope. It broke, I think. I'm not sure, but it gave way, and I started falling. Someone caught it." Blair hadn't known what state any of them were in. She blinked at Henry with a clear expression, unaware of her slight misdirection. He saw the question in Henry's raised brows—someone or something?

After Henry finished his questions, he continued to stare at them all. It was clear he didn't know what to ask to get the answers he knew were missing. For example, why the hell are all of you half naked and hiked all the way up here in your bare feet?

And the shifters didn't offer any explanations. Blair thought Tavis was right. They'd need to tell Henry, eventually. And she believed they could trust him. Deep down, she was sure they all believed it, too. But this wasn't a secret easy to divulge. Nor was it hers.

No one moved until Henry did. With a shaking head, he stood, giving them the non-verbal permission they needed to leave.

Blair closed her eyes and curled up against Noah on the ride down. The others said they didn't mind hiking, leaving the remaining side-by-side for them and Henry.

"I'll make sure both of your vehicles are brought here." Henry said as he dropped them off in front of Noah's house.

"Thanks, Henry." Noah gave a respectful nod, then carried her inside.

Any time she'd tried to apologize, Noah had shut her down, to wait until they were alone. He set her down on his couch and sat himself on the coffee table in front of her.

"Now, Blair."

"Nothing I say will be enough. I had only one thought. Get to Clara. It's one thing for me to throw myself out there, but it isn't right for others to get dragged into something they don't deserve. That's why I do what I do. I'm sorry, Noah. I lied when I made that promise. I knew it then. And I think you knew it too."

He nodded, his lips thin.

"I had time to at least call you and I didn't. I'm so sorry."

Noah didn't answer her right away. His jaw tightened and loosened as he looked down at the floor between their feet as if that space held the answers.

It was hard not to say something more to urge him to speak.

"I'm angry. I can't deny that." His voice was sharp enough to trigger her tears, but she held them back until he finished. "You're right. I knew that promise had been a lie. I need a new one, Blair. Not a lie this time. I can't—I won't lose you. And that is something that will take the two of us."

"This experience is making me question so many things. This went too far for me. I don't know what my career will look like from here. I'm still so scared, and the thought of writing this story or even another fills me with panic. I need time to see what will change in my future. But right now, I can safely say I will not run into known danger again without you by my side. I promise, wholeheartedly."

"And I will always be by your side, kitten. I promise, wholeheartedly." Noah leaned forward, sealing their lips in a scalding kiss. Her body heated and tingled with new life.

"I love you, Noah. I'm not leaving or going anywhere. I want to make this future work, no matter what sacrifices I have to make. I'm home. With you." Blair spoke, rushing every word over his lips.

"I love you too, kitten. You're home. I'm home. Marry me."

Not a question. Barely a plea. And mostly a demand that Blair wouldn't even try to fight. "Yes."

Noah moved to the side and slid his arms beneath her. Cradling her against him, he carried her to the master bathroom to set her on the counter.

"What are you doing?"

"A bath. You're sore."

He wasn't wrong. It was taking longer than she liked for her body to function again. She could stand and hold her weight, but her muscles and joints protested when she did.

Noah started the bath, then took her off the counter to strip her. "You're absolutely precious to me, Blair."

She accepted his light kisses as he peeled her clothes away. Once the bath was ready, he set her in the hot water and she groaned.

"Maybe a bigger bathtub is needed. And bubbles and salts on hand."

"You're a genius, bear man." Blair laid her head against the rim and closed her eyes. She concentrated on soaking in the heat.

Noah left her. It took a long time for the temperature in the water to drop, but the moment her body felt the change, her emotions rushed back like a flood.

She was safe, and Noah had forgiven her. But the weight of the disappointment still hurt. Her confidence turned into arrogance, putting her and others in danger.

How close she came to losing everything, losing her life and hurting Noah for life at her loss overwhelmed her.

"Aww, kitten. It's over." Rough fingers brushed away her tears. "This isn't something that will go away in a few hours or even days. It won't for me either."

Blair opened her eyes and turned her head to look at her mate. "I don't deserve such easy forgiveness from you."

His mouth started with a soft smile, but they tipped into something sinful. "It isn't easy forgiveness." His suggestive tone helped ease the tension.

His hand dipped into the water and down her belly. Fingers splayed through her core. She didn't have the strength to arch for more. Blair let him play, or punish, how he wanted.

She tried to turn her head, but his other hand gripped her chin.

"Mine, kitten." Noah pinched and rolled her clit, never looking away from her face and not allowing her to close her eyes. So much passed through his gaze. His hurt and anger. But his fear and panic that matched her own had a glow of its own. And finally, his love, his claim, his heart.

Her breath quickened the more he rolled and pinched. He didn't touch or do anything else. Pulling the pleasure forth, it balled itself in that one spot, ready for his command.

But he slowed and lifted his hand from the water. Blair kept her mouth shut, but she whimpered. That had been out of her control. She wouldn't beg. If this was something they needed to reconnect after almost losing everything, then she'd endure.

His nostrils flared and amusement replaced it all. Fun. Noah knew what they needed and Blair intended to trust him.

Tilting her chin up, he kissed her. It started harsh and filled with desire, but turned soft as he lifted her left hand up. When he pulled back, he slid a diamond ring on her finger.

Blair touched the square-cut gem. "You'd planned this?"

"I bought it the moment I found out you were my mate. I hadn't known how to overcome the secret and accept what Fate had planned, and despite fearing the pain of you leaving me, somewhere deep I knew the end would be like this."

He'd trusted it would work out.

Setting both her hands on his face, she pulled him down, surprising herself with her returning strength. His lips crashed against hers as he lost his grip on the edge, falling into the water with her.

They didn't break apart as they laughed, full and bellowing while water splashed across the bathroom floor.

"Oops," she said through her giggles, but his growl cut off her laughter.

"Bad kitten."

B lair lay stretched out beside him. Arms above her head and the sheets across her waist. Her eyelashes sat on her cheeks, content in slumber. She'd rested well through the night other than one moment where she cried out with the sensation of falling in her sleep.

For the past half an hour, she'd been stretching and sighing, her body readying itself to wake.

Well, Noah had a better idea.

Peeling the sheet off her waist, he moved with it to settle between her already spread legs without touching her.

His anger still simmered, but it would go away on its own. His trust in her on the other would take some time. But the only thing crossing his mind since he got her home last night had been that she was safe. Safe, in his arms, and all his.

Noah intended to celebrate that.

He ran his fingers up the side of her soft lips, pulling them apart. When he reached the hood hovering over the bundle of nerves, he pulled it back, startling a gasp from her. And that was the moment he latched on.

Lashing her clit with his tongue, he circled her entrance with a finger.

"Noah?"

He hummed and thrust his finger in. His intentions had been to tease her as he had in the tub. A bit of funishment. But he wasn't sure if he had the strength. It seemed like a waste of precious time together when instead he could give her an overabundance of pleasure.

Adding a second finger, he did just that. While he thrust, scissored, and spread, he sucked hard on her clit. Blair pulled on his hair and pushed her hips harder against him.

Fuck, she gave all she got. In everything. Not just here with him. And that was what made her so special. It's what made her foolishly jump to rescue someone she barely knew.

Knowing that was one reason he loved her helped ease more of his anger.

Curling his fingers inside her, he growled to get her attention. By the sound of it, his bear was there and ready for the fun too. Her wide eyes, still hazy with sleep, looked down her body. He trapped her gaze and tried to command her with a look, pushing the words through whatever connection they may have.

Come, kitten. Break apart and give me everything.

Blair gasped and her body trembled. She heard him. If not the words, then the intention. Thighs shaking, she came. Hard pulses squeezed his fingers.

Noah eased her down and with her last convulsion, he stopped. But only until the count of three, then he attacked. Lashing his tongue and filling her with his fingers.

Chuckling, he brought her to another quick climax. Her light scream was delicious to his ears, and tempting to force her to do it again. And again.

They had all the time in the world. No one expected them to emerge today. And he didn't plan on it.

By her third orgasm, her grip in his hair loosened. "Please, Noah."

"Please what, kitten?"

"Anything but that again."

He smiled against her while nipping across her skin, her thighs, over her mound and belly. "I suppose I can take pity on you."

Blair reached for him as he moved up her body, lining himself up with her core.

He wanted to repeat everything they'd said the night before. The promises, the vows, the demands. But there was no need. Her regret still flashed in her eyes, but so did her determination and her desire. The love they had for each other pulsed in the air, pulling at the magic between them.

Noah's teeth elongated as soon as he sank his cock into her heat. Her cry of ecstasy stirred his bear until he clawed to the front, shining through his eyes so he could see their mate at her most beautiful.

This was his life. She was his life.

Blair brought her knees up to his hips, opening herself to him.

"I love you, Noah. I hope I never give you reason to doubt that."

"You won't, kitten." His voice wasn't his own. "I love you."

She wasn't long reaching her climax. Her body tightened and quivered, holding herself on the edge after already having so many. Her body fought the next. She whimpered through the tortuous moment while Noah hammered harder to reach his own.

As soon as his built up, ready to explode, he gave them both permission to fall. Burying his face, he sank his teeth into his mate mark.

Magic filled him and ran through him. They both heated, warmth engulfing them in a cocoon while they experienced the height of pleasure.

It was as if Fate blessed them after giving them the time they needed to create their own bond.

Not until the last vestiges of their climaxes escaped did Noah pull his teeth free from her neck. Her breath shuddered from her.

"Mine," he murmured against her lips before kissing her back to life. Her hands fluttered over his shoulders.

"Yours. But that makes you mine, too."

"Always, kitten."

Epilogue

B lowing out a long breath between rounded lips, Blair straightened her shirt before knocking on the door.

It had been a week since she'd almost fallen to her death and she hadn't spoken to Clara. Blair apologized to Noah and again to Henry. She'd even apologized to Tavis. His warning about what Noah would lose if she was hurt had sunk in when he made it, but she saw the evidence of what Noah would go through over the past week. Blair hadn't been the only one waking in the night with nightmares.

But she hadn't apologized to Clara. If Blair hadn't antagonized Scott, he wouldn't have involved her, wouldn't have looked for a way to get to Blair.

The door opened a crack and Clara peeked around the edge. Her smile was small, but welcoming when she saw Blair.

"Hi. Can I come in?"

She nodded and opened the door wider. Blair stepped through to a house she'd already been in and now that felt like a violation.

"How are you doing? I'm not asking if you're okay, because I know that isn't true."

"I'm going back to work tomorrow. I need the routine." Clara led her to the couch.

"That's important and I'm missing that myself." Blair sat and stared at her fingers twisting together for a moment before meeting her eyes. "I'm so sorry."

Clara's eyes widened with shock. "*You're* sorry? Why are you apologizing?"

"He took you as a trap for me." Blair thought she'd known that.

She nodded. "But that doesn't mean it was your fault."

"I antagonized him. I shouldn't have."

Clara reached over and squeezed Blair's hand. "I don't blame you. That was all on them. I might have done some antagonizing of my own." She scrunched her nose and shrugged a shoulder.

Blair squeezed her hand back. "Still, I'm very sorry they dragged you into this."

"I think I was already in it. It felt like they were stalking me, following all of my classes."

"I think your classes have such a wide range that they were searching for someone who might be in one of them. You were a common denominator."

"You're probably right. Did they find the other one? Luca?"

"No." They'd tried to track him down, but he was gone. And the focus was more on Scott and not letting him escape. While Luca needed to pay too, Scott was the more dangerous one of the two. It was important he didn't escape again. No one believed Luca would return or even return to whatever job they'd been trying to complete.

"He stayed behind when the other guy came in here to take me." Now, Clara had a hard time looking up from her hands. "He didn't want to do it. But he didn't try too hard to stop him."

"No, he didn't." Luca had always been a pushover. And now he was in the wind. But at least he wouldn't cause any more problems, or so they believed. Blair didn't think he would on his own, but until she knew who had hired them and why, she wouldn't discount him entirely.

"How are you doing?" Clara leaned back further on the couch and twisted to face Blair.

"I'm doing. I have quite a bit of regret. I let a lot of people down. But I'm taking it day by day. I'm going back to the city to pack up my apartment and talk to my boss."

"Pack? You're moving to Firebrook?"

"Yes. This is home. Noah is my home."

Clara beamed. "That's wonderful. I wish you both the best."

"Thank you." Blair glanced at the coffee table. "Are those students?"

Clara picked up the pictures. "No. That's my nephew. He's ten and a handful. But so precious in our family."

Blair smiled at the pictures. "What's his name?"

"Kellan. He's insisted that my sister bring him by every day so he can help me."

"What a sweetheart."

"I'm going to be okay. Let go of your regret, Blair. None of this was your fault. This community will help both of us. My nephew won't have it any other way." She laughed through the stern expression a ten-year-old might use.

"I'm happy you have family here, too. But please call me if you need anything. I'd love it if we could become friends."

"I'd love that too."

Blair hugged Clara and said her goodbyes. Stepping out onto the street, she walked through town. People waved and smiled. Most she knew or recognized, some she didn't. But they knew her. Everyone knew her now.

Noah waited for her outside his house. Their house. Leaning against his truck, he had their two suitcases in the bed.

"Ready to go, kitten?"

"Yes." She was ready to pack up her old life and settle into her new one. Her new home.

Pressing herself against Noah, she stood on her toes to kiss him. Blair planned to kiss him every chance she had. Never again would she give him a chance to doubt her.

Turned out Fate really did know what she was doing.

Wedding season was busy in Firebrook. More so when the wedding was for someone in the community. Wyatt and Poppy had been planning this for longer than some had expected. To the community it had looked like a whirlwind romance and people had been speculating on the nuptials since Poppy returned to claim her love for one of the Greer men.

Tavis stayed clear of almost everything wedding related, but since the groom was one of his cousins, that wasn't possible. The wedding party had arrived two days ago and today was the day that the entire community would gather in the centre of town.

They'd decided on an open wedding, closing out the summer season with a bang. There were some specific invitations sent, and those seats were reserved. The rest of the public could fill the remaining seats or stand in the park.

Tavis helped with setting up, with decorating, and everything bachelor related. But *Rockhard Bears* had also kept him busy aside from wedding events. He was exhausted and had slept through rehearsal the night before. It wasn't the first wedding he'd seen or been in. He knew how to walk in a straight line and smile.

Expectations of how hectic the wedding day was were lower than they should have been.

Waiting at the lodge with Wyatt and the other groomsmen, his brother and cousin, Tavis lounged on the couch with a whiskey in his hand. The others did the same. They were waiting for the photographer.

May, the one friend of Poppy's who hadn't come with them on their first trip to Firebrook. But she wouldn't miss the wedding. And refused to let anyone else photograph it.

"No one is good enough for my best friend but me." Her voice had rung with confidence over the speaker when Poppy had called to ask her to be a bridesmaid. Tavis had walked in for dinner that evening during her call with her friends. Her sweet sound carrying a husky rasp that had stirred something in him he'd been happy to shake off after the phone call had ended.

Tavis hadn't met her yet. During all the wedding preparations and events, they'd never crossed paths. And in his gut it felt like anticipation.

As soon as she walked through the door, he understood why. While the others all set their drinks down and stood, Tavis gripped his glass tighter and froze.

The pixie with shoulder length hair bounced into the room with her camera around her neck and snapped an instant picture, laughing all the while. She'd pinned her hair back in a half up-do, pink stripes woven through the curls of her dark hair.

"Candids are important." She looked at each of them, but when her eyes reached Tavis, still sitting, she shivered.

Yeah, pixie. You're mine. His mate was the best friend of his cousin's and brother's mates and the photographer of the wedding. Her scent of sweet cherries rooted him to the couch. But the others were already moving outside for the pictures, walking past May, who still stared at him.

Tavis didn't want to break the moment.

Her breathing turned shallow, and she lifted her camera. He didn't move while she snapped a picture, then lowered her camera again.

"You must be Tavis."

He nodded. "And you're May."

"I..." Her hand fluttered over her belly.

Tavis forced himself out of the stupor and set his drink down. He stalked toward her, offering his arm. "Shall we?"

May nodded and set her small hand on his arm. They both gasped, but took their first steps outside.

The next several hours had a hazy magic about them. Stolen smiles and looks between him and his mate kept his attention riveted. He barely remembered the ceremony or the food he ate at the reception.

But he remembered every smile and laugh that came from May.

The first stars shone above the lit park covered in cream coloured light, greenery and bright flowers. And the music flowed for everyone to enjoy.

Tavis walked over to where she sat, speaking with Blair. Instead of standing over her, he crouched down to look into her eyes.

"Would you like to dance?"

Her teeth pulled at her bottom lip, and she nodded. Holding out his hand, he clasped his fingers around hers and pulled her up as he stood as well.

Leading her to the dance floor put butterflies in his stomach. A sensation he hadn't felt since his first kiss in middle school, thinking that was the culmination of the feelings he'd ever experience. But this right now was only the beginning. He couldn't wait to feel what the rest of their firsts were like.

He pulled and spun his mate toward him, his hand settling at the small of her back, and he held her hand against his chest.

Words caught in his throat. *Lovely wedding. I can't wait to see the pictures. You're beautiful.*

Her eyes danced with similar words, but they only moved around the dance floor in small circles.

Tavis didn't know what she knew. Had Poppy told all her friends about shifters? Blair had known. He suspected Harlyn, their other friend that had come with them on their first visit, knew. But May had been spared from all of that.

"I want to kiss you, pixie."

"Pixie?" Her head reared back, but she laughed.

He let his intention through with his own grin. "Yeah. Pixie. I think it's the hair." The pink stripes got to him.

"Is that a bad thing or a good thing?" She tilted her head, and he swore she even moved a little closer.

"A good thing. A very good thing." Tavis matched her movement.

"So, you want to kiss me, eh?" There was a slight country twang in her voice and he wondered what her upbringing had been like. She didn't look like a farm girl right now, but that didn't mean she hadn't been.

"Yes, I want to kiss you." He lowered his voice and leaned close enough their breaths mingled. "I want to taste you."

"Then do it." Her lips parted and her eyes stayed on his, challenging him to follow through.

Setting her hand on his shoulder, he used his to run his fingers over her cheek and down her neck. "I think *pixie* was the right choice for you."

She smiled until his lips touched hers. His heart hammered against his ribs and he felt hers beat incessantly. His blood boiled and his cock throbbed. There was no hiding the bulge that pressed against her belly.

They hadn't needed that kiss to start their bond as mates. Tavis had to remind himself they were in the middle of a crowded dance floor, so he didn't take things too far. His fingers splayed on her back until his pinkie touched the top of her ass and his other hand cupped the side of her neck.

When he lifted his head, her eyes were wide and glassy.

"I could make some really bad decisions with you, Tavis."

He laughed. "You and me both, pixie."

Join my newsletter to keep up to date on new releases, special events, and sneak peeks.
https://bit.ly/3oTgH5u
Also, visit my website at...
http://www.authorsarahurquhart.com
... to see my full book list.

Don't want to miss out on **Stormy Rescue**, Book Three in the Fire-brook Bears series? Follow me so you don't miss out on any updates!
Instagram: https://www.instagram.com/authorsarahu/
Reader Group: https://www.facebook.com/groups/sarahswildon
es
Facebook: https://www.facebook.com/authorsarahu
BookBub: https://www.bookbub.com/profile/sarah-urquhart

Wild Rescue, Firebrook Bears Book One

He won't take what he can't keep.
Poppy Mackenzie thinks she's happy. Sure, not everything has gone her way. She has a non refundable vacation that she's not willing to give up with her ex. She never noticed the rage hiding under his surface until her vacation takes a turn off a cliff.
Wyatt Greer picks up her irresistible scent on a search and rescue. His life in Firebrook is full with his lodge and the mountains which doesn't leave room for a brassy city bartender. But Fate knows what she's doing when she throws his mate into his life.

Sweet Abandon, A Firebrook Novella tells the story of Bonnie and Easton. **Free** eBook from your favourite retailer.
https://books2read.com/firebrooknovella

Firebrook Bears Series
Sweet Abandon - Novella
Wild Rescue
Rocky Rescue
Stormy Rescue
Tangled Rescue
Wounded Winds Series
White Bonds
Auburn Ties
Silver Chains
Amber Oath
Emerald Promise
Golden Vow

Looking at a crossroads, Sarah chose to write. With a deep love of anything romance, it was natural that romance stories flowed into her journal.

From the East Coast and living in Alberta, Canada, she enjoys life with her family and the beauty of the province around her. She gets hilariously excited when new stories and characters pop in her head and can't wait to write them out whether in the sub-genres of romantic suspense or paranormal romance.

She hopes her readers enjoy her stories as much as she enjoys writing them.

www.ingramcontent.com/pod-product-compliance
Lightning Source LLC
Chambersburg PA
CBHW030823210726
48290CB00002B/727